MW00930301

Notes:

NOTES:

If you find any typos or errors in the book, please report them to me at yourrobotoverlord3500@gmail.com, and I will try to fix them.

All characters appearing in this are fictitious. Any resemblance to actual persons, living or dead, is purely coincidental.

Updated on 11/20/2024 (typo)

Many thanks to my Reviewers:

- Christie Marston
- John Donigan
- Keith Verret

The Repulser Grid Pattern

1 + 6 + 12 + 18 + 24 = 61

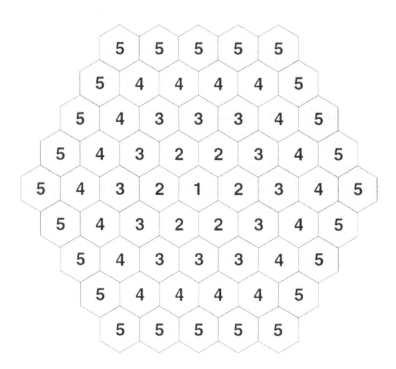

Earlier Story:

This is the fourth book in the "Wars Without End" series.

#1 The 2,000 Year War

An underemployed technician accepts an online job application for an out-of-this-world (literally) position and finds himself now in a pivotal role in a war between multiple alien races. A war that has gone on for over 2,340 years.

#2 The Second War

The accidental hero now has to deal with new aliens and discovers that not all aliens fit into a simple good or bad role. What should have been an upgrade to the old ship that served him so well in the first story has unexpected and potentially devastating consequences.

#3 The Convention War

After being dropped off at Comic-Con with a number of his alien crew, the ship faces several more new aliens. One group turns out to be more victims of the Meduala. The second is a survivor of a race that was supposed to be blasted back to the Stone Age; they missed one. The last has them discovering several solar systems made entirely out of antimatter. A place where a single grain of sand could lead to instant thermonuclear annihilation.

PROLOGUE:

[Markonon Cheasobod]

Commander, I have awakened you from your stasis chamber. I have detected a weak radar ping. An unknown massive ship has exited FTL approximately one light hour from us. They are just sitting there. They are possibly making repairs. Like us, they may have struck contrary-matter. The ship is massive. It does not match any configuration we have on our records."

"How long have we sat in this patched-up shuttle crammed full of stasis pods?"

"I show the elapsed time as over 800 years. The projected maximum life of the stasis pods is less than 1,000 years. All of our pods are still operational. However, I predict that one will start to fail within fifty years."

"Leave the others in stasis for now. Can you send a response to the other ship?"

"The transmitter is still operational. The shuttle drive is non-repairable."

"Start signaling them with whatever we have that they won't misinterpret it as a weapon's discharge."

"What should I say?"

"Doesn't matter. The ship is unknown. They are probably aliens."

"If they are hostile?"

"Then we die, the same as if they don't notice us and the power cells run empty, or the stasis consumables run out, or we get a hole in the hull and lose all the air."

"Commander, this shuttle hull already has a slow leak and no longer holds any air. I may be able to refill the hull once, but it will vent to vacuum in only six hours."

"Send the universal surrender signal. Hopefully, it doesn't translate into alien as something stupid like, 'I just ate your grandmother's liver.'"

CAUTION

One Hour earlier:

The starship, the Lunalily, exited FTL in the middle of nowhere and did the routine scans.   Nothing showed up.

"Luna, send out the strongest Q-band radar pulses you can; try and ensure nothing is out here.   I don't want to accidentally find so much as an antimatter grain of dust."

"Rotating the ship, sending out max strength pulses, and setting the receiver to the highest gain.   We should be able to detect anything out there using these settings.

… … …

Ten minutes later, Luna reported, "I did a lot of directional scans. We are clear of anything I can detect in a five-light second range. That is almost three times the distance to the moon.   We should be safe.   I am sending the drones out to start the installation of the antigravity repulsers."

… … …

Two hours later, Luna reported, "Captain, I have a Shuttle-sized target.   Distance is about one light hour.   That is far too distant for detecting any thermal signature or power signature.   The object is only showing up on the Q-band radar."

"Continue monitoring while working on your new repulser matrix. Don't send any more Q-band pulses until we are almost ready to jump to FTL."

Jennifer Woods said, "Poop, I hate mentioning this, but it could be another antimatter-ship.   We are between two stars; one is matter, and the other is antimatter.   We are closer to the matter star; this ship didn't come from that star. It has no viable planets in its Goldilocks zone."

"How much protection will seven repulsers provide?"

Luna said, "Enough to sweep away gaseous molecules, but not enough to keep larger dust particles away. For that, we need at least nineteen repulsers. It would take four more days to print that many and another day to install them all."

"And if you had all sixty-one?"

"Reasonably safe from most things smaller than a BB in front of the ship and probably out the sides to twelve degrees."

Anderson said, "That sounds worth the delay and the extra power issues."

Luna said, "Seven will be enough to make it safe to get close enough to determine if they are made from matter or antimatter. Nothing we do makes it safe if they are antimatter."

"How do we determine what they are made of?"

Jennifer Woods said, "Determining what they are made of is easy. Having them survive the test is the trickier part. Flip a coin, heads, we rescue you; tails, you have exploded."

.. .. ..

When we had seven repulsers operational, we did a micro-FTL hop and put ourselves at a distance of 1.5 light seconds—the distance from the Earth to the moon.

I said, "First test, Luna, see if they respond to any Q-band or old-style radio. I think we want to avoid the tap and explode test if possible."

They responded with a low-speed data link after only five minutes of testing. Then we sat back and waited while the link slowly increased and Luna and the other ship's computer figured out how to talk to each other. This was slow, and we spent almost three hours before Luna announced, "We have a vocal translation working; vocabulary will be limited, and the syntax is sketchy. So far, I have only talked to the AI, which is not all that sophisticated. It is putting on what roughly translates as the Captain. Starting link now, you are up."

I said, "This is Captain Keith Robinson, on the United Federation starship, the Lunalily. Are you in need of assistance?"

Three seconds later, A male voice replied, "This is Captain Cheasobod of the Forandicate. We are in a shuttle, serving as a makeshift lifeboat. The three remaining crew are in survival pods. The engine is disabled, and the hull has a slow leak. We were not aware of the contrary nature of the matter of some stars in this area. We ask for assistance. If you are a military vessel, we surrender unconditionally."

Luna said, "I am guessing on his title, Captain should be close."

"We represent a large collection of different races. This is not a military ship, but we do have representatives of the Earth military on board. Do you have video capability?"

Luna said, "Limited video; shall I enable it?"

"Yes."

The main screen lit up to show a cramped pod with a large clear window, and behind it were several other large cylindrical chambers crammed into it. The individual on the screen looked like a human, except that its ears were like elf ears, only they stuck out sideways and were decorated with multiple piercings and strange inserts in the ears. The nose and mouth were almost human-looking, and the eyes were the most striking difference. It had three of them arranged in a triangle.

Luna said, "I am approximating with their units, but he appears to be just over five feet tall."

We introduced ourselves.

"I am Keith Robinson, a male of the human species. I am also the captain of the Lunalily ship."

"I am Jake Anderson, another male, also of Earth, and I represent the Earth's military and governments."

"I am Dariea Fenagol Resonon, a female of the species Fezzcoll."

"I am Jennifer Woods, a female of the species human and the ship's science officer."

"I am Trishah Maconda of the Sulimon race, also a female."

"I am Dariea Fenagol Resonon, a female of the Fezzcoll race."

"Marnia-12, of the Prolozar race, female."

"I am Princess Domonis of the Meduala race, and I am a female."

I said, "We have a few other races on the ship, but these are the primary command crew members."

Captain Cheasobod said, "I would introduce my other crew, but they are not awake in their chambers.   The most important question, and one that I never expected to ask, is, what type of matter are you composed of?   My ship reports that you are staying a safe distance away."

Luna said. "I am Luna, the AI on this ship.   Determining the material composition of your ship is the tricky part.   We know of a ship made of contra-matter, but due to their low technology level, it will take them months to reach you. If you are contra-matter, we can not help you.   They are your only help."

"How do you determine what our ship is composed of?"

"We can detect a minor shift in the hydrogen spectral bands, and we are using that to determine what type of star it is.   Unfortunately, your ship has no detectable hydrogen. For ships, well, there is the explosive test."

"For obvious reasons, we would rather avoid that test.   How small of an object can you detect?"

"For metallic, we can detect anything larger than 1/5000 of the length of your shuttle."

"You have exceptional sensors; I will have the ship reposition the antennas, which usually breaks some ice and dust free; please wait."

.. .. ..

Three minutes later, Luna reported, "I have detected particles; most are drifting close to your ship's relative velocity. One chunk of ice is sublimating, but assuming the gas particles follow a normal course, I can have a probe intercept it at what should be a safe distance. For your ship, it will be safe; the probe will not survive if it is contra matter. Most of the debris from the probe will be directed away from your ship. If any does go your way... Your death should be quick..."

"Please position your probe; quick is preferable to our current condition. We are rapidly depleting the stasis consumables and losing power."

.. .. ..

"The probe is in position, and the projected gas cloud will reach it in three minutes...."

At that moment, the probe exploded like a miniature nuclear bomb."

Luna said, "That was an impact on the far side of the probe; the remaining probe debris is heading to your ship. This is most unexpected. It did not fit the projection models."

"How long until impact?"

"Fifteen more seconds."

"I should have woken my crew, but perhaps it will be better if they sleep through it. Thank you for trying."

.. .. ..

"I am hearing pinging and small thuds. There is debris hitting our ship, but it is not contra-matter."

"We are between two stars; the closer one is matter, the other is antimatter. I suspect we encountered antimatter dust, but that your ship is normal matter. It should be safe to rescue you. It is most definitely not safe to remain here. Do you agree to be rescued by our ship?"

"Please do; I hope you have air we can breathe and that our microbes are not aggressively parasitic to each other."

"You show 17.1% oxygen, 82.3% nitrogen, and 0.6% carbon dioxide as the main ingredients.   That is tolerable for us; we prefer more oxygen and less carbon dioxide."

"It sounds like we are compatible…   Yikes, your ship just appeared in front of us.   It did it without an obvious FTL bubble flare.   It's also huge!"

Luna said, "Your ship will fit within the cargo bay; please wait."

We were all a little bit nervous, okay, a fricking lot nervous loading the derelict shuttle.   Luna made sure to vent some gasses at the ship when we were at a safe distance just to triple-check that it wasn't antimatter.

After it was loaded, we pressurized the compartment, and Captain Cheasobod had to adjust their pressure to avoid any issues; they spent twenty minutes equalizing their pressure.

Luna spent the time talking to Captain Cheasobod and improving the language translation.   During that time, he had the three additional crew wake up in their stasis pods.   Finally, it was time for them to exit the ship.

THE FORANDICATE

When they exited the ship, they were somewhat bent over and cramped from the tight space that had managed to fit four stasis pods into one shuttle. They had also ripped out all the seats.

The first one spoke, "I am Captain Cheasobod... Or I was; this is only a non-functional shuttle lifeboat. I suppose I am now just Markonon Cheasobod, former commander of the ship the Far-Singer and perhaps the first of the Forandicate to have their ship come in contact with antimatter. My rank in the military is O-3, [Captain]; I am also a male."

"I am Chisai Cheasobod, I hold the rank O-2 [First Lieutenant], I am female and the second wife... Crap, I am now the only surviving wife, so I suppose I am now Markonon's first wife."

Markonon said, "Our ship originally contained a crew of seventeen; the shuttle only holds four."

"I am Laido Severit, of the rank E-5 [Sargent]. I was in charge of Navigation and piloting, but we had never expected to encounter contra-matter. Oh, I am also male."

"I am Zenner Cheasobod, rank E-2 [Private], the Captain's niece. I was a biologist studying alien life forms. I had not completed my official education. If I had, I would have been automatically promoted to O-1 [Second Lieutenant]."

I asked, " Is it common to have family relationships between crews of what seems like a military ship?"

"The ship, the Far-Singer, had been out for twenty-two Prime-orbits [twenty-four years]. My niece was born after the ship left our home planet. Laido was the son of a civilian contractor and was only sixteen Prime-orbits [seventeen years] old when we left. After the ship was disabled, we cobbled the shuttle into a lifeboat. We fit four stasis pods in it. The main ship has six others in stasis pods, and those not in stasis pods have long since perished. If possible, I would like you to attempt to recover any other survivors from the main ship."

14

Luna said, "I am in discussion with the shuttle AI; their ship was not FTL capable, and it has been drifting for 800 Prime-orbits. I think we can find it within two or three days, but the antimatter in the area remains a problem. That time unit equates to 873 Earth years. It may not still be there."

At that point, Laido collapsed to his knees.

"I am sorry. The stasis may have delayed the effects of the radiation, but it has accumulated while you slept."

I said, "We have medical chambers; they may be able to reverse some of the damage. They can keep you awake while making repairs. You may want to enter the chambers, and then we will wake you up if… I mean, when we find your ship…"

"If may be the correct term; also, your translation is working remarkably well for so little time."

Luna said, "I am giving a lot of the credit to the AI on your shuttle. While inefficient, the way they stored vocabulary lends itself well to translations."

"Unfortunately, the linguistics expert and the software engineers were some of those that stayed on the main ship."

Zenner Cheasobod then passed out and landed hard on the floor.

"I think we will now take the offered medical assistance. I hope they work."

THE FAR-SINGER

[Markonon Cheasobod]

I awoke in a strange chamber, and this was not the stasis chamber I had spent so much time in.

The new ship's AI voice said, "Good afternoon, Captain Cheasobod. Three days have passed, and we have located the remains of your ship. How extensive was the damage when you left it?"

"The engines were mostly intact; they were at the aft end. The bridge area was almost completely destroyed in the initial accident, and then a secondary explosion occurred, venting all the main ship's fuel. The reactor was intact, so we had power. Unfortunately, all of our communications equipment was on the bridge, as well as my first wife. We spent two weeks readying the shuttle as a lifeboat. During that time, there were no additional explosions, but we did characterize the source of the explosions."

Luna said, "Until recently, we had never encountered natural antimatter other than as random gas particles. An antimatter ship, probably less advanced than you were, showed up at a normal matter star, and it didn't end well for that ship or the survey ship it encountered. The damage doesn't seem to be worse than what you described. I detect a functional power signature, probably your reactor. I am preparing space suits for you and your crew. We will have them ready in a few minutes. The last item is what color they should be to be recognized as a rescue attempt. Once you are in, I assume you will remove your helmets and speak the language. Unfortunately, the docking adapter will not be compatible. You will need to enter manually through an airlock."

"That should be fine. I only need suits for myself, First Lieutenant Chisai Cheasobod, and Sargent Laido Severit. My niece doesn't need to see what we may find. Our stasis pods were not the most reliable, and using them was not a guarantee of survival."

All of us were ejected at the same time from the medical pods. The AI reported that all of us had minor radiation poisoning cleared up. Chisai also had a second degree burn cleared up on her back and shoulder.

The three of us going to the ship were ushered to changing rooms, where we were provided with hard spacesuits.

"Wow, they are impressive, and you said you produced these in only a few days?"

"We have a generic suit design that only needs minor changes to work with several different races. You fit in a human design. The only thing I had to change was that more of the helmet needed to be transparent, and the helmet is a little wider than for humans to fit your ears. The three eyes are a different trait from the other races. We do have one race that has extra limbs."

Then, we were led to the hangar, and the AI explained the operation of the shuttle. All we had to do was tell it what we wanted it to do. The AI took care of operating the shuttle. The three of us sat in the shuttle and were mostly silent for the ride.

Change course, head to the aft section, and rotate to the top. The other way, if the front of the ship were intact, the top would be more obvious.

.. .. ..

"There, the area with a circle marked around it. That is a manual airlock hatch." We exited the shuttle and drifted over to the derelict.

"I don't know how you do that artificial gravity, but it is wonderful." It took us a few minutes to readjust to zero gravity. "Is everyone okay?"

"Yeah."

"For now."

"Crap, it shows as zero pressure on the other side. This is an airlock, and it should be pressurized. I am opening the outer door. It is working, but it is stiff, almost... I have it open; all three of us should fit.   I show pressure on the other side of the inner door, but it is low, about 15% of normal. It may have a very slow leak."

I closed the inner door.

In the distance, I heard several alarms, but they were muffled sounding.

Zenner said, "Should I silence the alarms?"

"When we get to a data terminal, assuming it still works, have it display what the alarms were for. Hopefully, none are for radiation or anything like that."

He went over to the first terminal.

"Pressure low, hard faults of too many things to read off, all located in the front of the ship. I can pause the alarms, but hard faults automatically reset after thirty-two minutes.   Crap, one of the stasis chambers has failed.   I don't know yet who was in that one. I show that one ran out of chemicals, but the occupant is still somehow alive. We need to get to that one now. The others are… The chambers are in the central room.   I am unable to add more air to the ship. The air reserves are completely depleted.   Chamber B2 is the one that is out of consumables."

I said, "We will take the two chambers that show the most critical and move them to the airlock."

The AI spoke, "The second ship followed you, and all the seats in that one have been stowed. It should fit four of your chambers, but we don't have a compatible power hookup.   Do they have battery backups?"

I said, "Yes, but I wouldn't trust them to work as old as they are. We have two that are reporting their status as critical."

"I have read your data files or at least the open documents; I believe they will be okay without power for twenty minutes, even if the batteries are depleted.   With your units, that is twenty-four ciisons."

We started the disconnect operations in parallel when they were both physically disconnected. We removed the power connections.

One lit up, saying the battery was good for 700 ciisons. The other only read forty-five ciisons, and the number started dropping quickly.

"The ship is at zero gravity, and the pods are disconnected, get moving. We need to get these two over before we return and start on the others. We should be able to move the pods in zero gravity."

The AI said, "I have drones ready to assist; if they are ejected from the stasis pod, how long until they wake up?"

"Probably ten or fifteen ciisons. Record my voice and play it if they start to wake up."

I spoke in our language, "**You are being transferred to a medical pod. Do not resist. The stasis pod was failing.**"

"I hope that works. I also hope they survive."

The display changed on the stasis pod with the failed battery.

"Run, we need this in a shuttle with air in it. The battery fell to critical, and it started the wake-up sequence. The last part of the wake-up sequence is the chamber door opening, and we are still in a vacuum."

We started running while carrying a stasis pod that weighed as much as several adults. It may now be weightless, but it had inertia, and we were bouncing off the walls.

Laido yelled, "Arrgh, my hand, I think my suit is holding air, but I think I crushed my fingers."

I yelled, "Get the drones over here. We need their help."

The first of the drones entered, and it clamped onto the stasis pod and started maneuvering it out of the ship a lot faster than we had been.

"Laido, follow and head back with them; your suit may start leaking anytime."

The AI reported, "His suit is already leaking, but the amount is not a problem at this time. He is bleeding, and it is freezing as it exits his glove. This may damage his hands severely if he doesn't get the suit removed as soon."

The first of the stasis pods was in the ship when the pod reported it was starting the unlock sequence. The ship slammed the door down, with just the one pod in it, and did a hard repressurization.

The AI reported, "The second pod and the injured crewman must now be moved to the second shuttle. We will return to the ship at that point. I think the drones can handle the additional pod extractions. Do you have a voltmeter or a device to measure voltage?"

"Yes, yes, we have those; I can get one from the utility panel. Why?"

"We need to verify the voltage units before we attempt to make an adapter to power your pods during transportation. I believe we can get the other pods without the panicky rush if we make an adapter."

I headed inside, only to find a drone was already extracting another stasis pod.

"The battery was reading 700 ciisons remaining, and only fifteen have gone by; this has now dropped to 470 ciisons remaining. None of the batteries are holding up."

I followed the pod to the second shuttle. I felt a bit useless; I was the commander, and the alien drones were doing a better job than we had done at rescuing my crew. I decided to follow it. The drones may be able to extract the pods better than we did, but the real chore is convincing my people to accept the new reality. Hopefully, the aliens can return us home. I hope our people don't shoot first when this massive ship shows up. Assuming we survived that long...

WAKING THE CREW

[Keith Robinson]

Luna said, "The extraction of the first two alien survival stasis pods went tolerably well. One patient was emergency ejected, and the ship managed to get air in the shuttle before the hatch opened. They were docking in the shuttle bay when he woke up. We kept repeating the words from the captain, and the patient stayed in the chamber. Then, the second chamber was opened, then Captain Cheasobod was there for the patient. The first one was Midder Frochis, a male, and his rank was E-3. He had some medical issues and would need to spend close to a week in a medical pod. The stasis pod running out of reactants and exposing him to low pressure caused a lung to puncture. The second one was a female named Lena Motoko; she was of rank E-2 and had no issues, but only as her chamber was in slightly better shape."

"Are we sending Captain Cheasobod out with the next recovery crew?"

"Yes, but only him. Laido Severit will remain in a medical chamber for about eighteen hours. He didn't fully break the bones, but he came as close as you can. Their bones have a secondary elastic reinforcing. The outer hard layer is cracked, and the inner membrane holds it together. I am evaluating if this is a modification we can make available for the Marines. It probably has some downsides, but it makes bones almost like safety glass. The pieces stay in almost the right place."

Marnia-12 wandered it at that point. She sniffed the air a bit. "These aliens smell like prey and not predators or omnivores."

"What do you mean?"

"They look like predators; they have eyes close together and facing forward, even if they have that creepy extra one, but they smell like a herd animal and prey."

"What about humans?"

"You are omnivores, meat, and plants. I can tolerate cooked meat, but I prefer mine raw. What do they eat?"

Luna said, "So far, they have not eaten in front of us. When they were in the medical pod, I analyzed the residual excrement from their digestive systems. All the material I found was replicator-created and plant-based."

"Are any of the other races herbivores?"

"It is about 60% carnivore and 35% omnivore. The only herbivores are the Prebelates."

"Oh them, the willing slaves of the Fezzcoll. I have not seen any of those since we left Potolul-2."

Luna said, "Even the Pargaina, the poor bastards derived from the Pargo and stuck for 2,000 years in a ship, ate vat-grown meat and fish. They are now happily converting to full carnivores."

"Why?"

"They love meat, and that is being used as a carrot by the Pargo to get them to convert back to normal bodies. Hee hee… Snicker… A meat carrot…"

"Are there any issues with the new race being herbivores?"

"Would you want your young raised by a pride of lions? They may feel like that is what is happening."

"Probably not, but we do have some people who raise large cats as pets."

"Oh, I would so do that. Then we could all go on a hunt and bring down some tasty prey."

"Yeah, now I can see where that may make them nervous. I thought the Prolozar were omnivores?"

"Not by choice, the station replicators made most of our food, and we supplemented that with greenhouse-grown vegetables and the occasional cage-grown fribbits."

I knew what those were; several alien races had those on their menu. In Peru, they serve Cuy, cooked guinea pigs. The aliens ate something very similar, only it was alive and kicking when they ate it. Some prefer it fresh but not moving. If the new aliens are herbivores, watching the carnivores eat live animals may be a bit much.

"Luna, send the captain over here; I want to discuss potential dietary differences between the races."

"Captain Cheasobod has returned to a medical pod to complete his earlier treatment. I can eject him in seventy-three minutes. If I need to force eject him now, his treatment will be extended, and he will be in some discomfort."

"No, that is fine; it can wait."

"Chisai Cheasobod, his wife, can be ejected in thirty minutes, or Zenner Cheasobod, his niece, can be ejected now. Alternatively, they can be woken up in ten minutes, and I can have them speak to you while they are in the medical pod."

"Eject his niece. How is she doing with the language packs?"

"Ejecting her now, she is about the best of the first four. The new ones won't be done with medical and language for a few days. The one that ran out of stasis chemicals will be there for three additional days. That severely damaged the organ that serves the same function as your liver."

"Biologically, are they omnivores or herbivores?"

"Herbivores. They need to eat a lot of grasses and grains, but they also eat insects."

"Great, do we have any vegetarians in the crew… Let me guess, Jennifer Woods?"

"Surprisingly, she is an omnivore; she, like several of the crew, attempts to eat a lot of vegetables, but more for diet and weight loss, then they order a steak when they see it on the menu. We do have several of the crew that are real vegetarians. None of the military people, mostly the scientists. Doctor Cora Smith almost qualifies as a vegetarian. She gets easily swayed by anything with bacon on it. So salad with bacon bits, baked potato, with bacon bits and sour cream..."

"Stop it. If you keep listing those foods, I will be drooling and heading to the cafeteria."

"Zenner Cheasobod is on her way to the conference room. And Marnia-12 is on her way to the cafeteria. I will distract and keep her out of your hair until after you have your discussion with Zenner."

Two minutes later, Zenner Cheasobod arrived at the conference room. The only other occupant was Trishah Maconda, one of the Sulimon. She was using the data terminal in the corner, reviewing some data.

Trishah said, "I will be quiet, Captain. I am reviewing the data on their ship's damage. Something about the damage is not adding up correctly."

Zenner arrived, and she did what was probably some type of military salute. It was an odd one, with a closed fist, fingers pointing down against the neck.

"Greeting Zenner, or should I call you by your full name or by your rank? This is not a military ship, but we have some crew affiliated with several military groups. We are classified as a civilian ship but one with some military capabilities."

"Greeting Captain Robinson. The proper way to greet someone in the Forandicate military is by rank and last name. So you would address me as Private Cheasobod, and you may add my first name if others of my family are present. Using the first name alone is more for family or intimate friends."

"Okay, Private Cheasobod. I would have summoned your uncle, the captain, but something has come to my attention, and I would like to informally discuss it if that is acceptable."

"Is there a problem with some of the crew who are being transferred to the medical pods?"

"No, it is a potential cultural issue. Feel free to discuss this with your uncle after the meeting."

"Err, I guess that is acceptable; what is the issue?"

"This ship, and most of the races in the Federation of Worlds and the Meduala, are composed of races that are either omnivores or carnivore species. Biologically, the Forandicate appears to be herbivores. While on this ship, most of the food is synthesized and created in replicators, but much is based on animals originally. We can replicate food that will be edible for you. Still, we would rather avoid any cultural taboos and can set up a separate dining facility for you and your crew if our dining habits are unpleasant to you."

"Oh, thank you. We have already observed several of the different races consuming food. We have attempted to be polite and ignore it, but it was unsettling."

"What are your normal foods? Please let the AI know, and we will set up a food replicator for you. Also, how about the gravity?"

"The artificial gravity is a little lower than our home planet, but we have… Or had when last we had contact with them, set up colonies of three other worlds. Two were very close to this gravity. One was stronger than our home world. Needless to say, that one was not very popular. We eat grasses, fruits and berries, green leafy material, and lots of ferns. We also consume small quantities of insects mixed in with our food, and trilitots are a staple."

"The last word did not translate."

"Oh, insects that have a hard outer shell of calcium. We need the shells for developing bones."

Luna said, "I have found these in the ship's database."

An image of a land-based hermit crab appeared on the screen. Then, a ruler appeared beside it and showed that they were much smaller than I initially thought; they were less than an inch long.

Luna said, "We don't have many insects in the replicator database, but we do have shellfish from either freshwater or saltwater."

An image appeared next to the trilitots showing a crayfish. It was maybe 50% longer than their native insect."

"These are bottom-dwelling crustaceans that live underwater."

Then, the image changed and showed a snail.

"These are land-based gastropods, separate from insects. We also have water-based versions of them. We have a replicator database version for both of these."

"It sounds like you can produce some foods that meet our dietary requirements. Our former ship-based foods were… Well, less than desired."

"We plan to bring over the remaining surviving crew from your ship. The drones are performing that task. They should have them over here and in medical pods within twenty-four hours. Most of your crew should only require a few days in the medical pods. The next step is getting you set up for food. This ship is quite large. And we expect that those still in stasis pods should survive. We will outfit some of your crew with spacesuits and allow you to recover any artifacts you want. This ship's AI has gained access to your ship's AI, and we have translated many of the data files. This is the fringes of the area we consider the Federation of Worlds. After your crew is recovered and everyone is walking around, then we can discuss eventually returning you to your space. You are military-based, so we would rather avoid causing a disturbance by showing up with a massive ship that they mistake as a warship. Did your race have quantum communicators?"

"Yes, we did. Unfortunately, those were in the front portion of the ship… The part that is missing. They needed to be created as matched pairs so we cannot reestablish long-range communications with our home world. I will let my uncle, the captain, know."

DAMAGE

Five days later, we had a meeting in the conference room. In it were me, Marnia-12, Jennifer Woods, Dariea Fenagol Resonon, Jake Anderson, Trishah Maconda, Princess Domonis, Captain Cheasobod, and his wife, First Lieutenant Cheasobod.

I said, "Luna, give us a status update."

"The surviving crew of the Far-Singer are all on board, and all but two have completed all their medical treatments. They have filled three shuttles with salvage artifacts from their old ship. The most important of them was an H-band communication radio. We will hopefully be able to communicate with their homeworld using it. The food replicators have been set up, and long-term staples from the ship have been entered into the replicators. Feeding them and keeping them alive should not be an issue. The production of the repulser grid is progressing, and we now have thirty-seven active repulsers. The final configuration will be sixty-one repulsers."

First Lieutenant Cheasobod asked. "What are the repulsers?"

"The rescue we did before finding you was to warn a different race away from the star system they were heading toward. They developed on a star system made entirely of antimatter. The best we could do was establish radio communications and warn them away. We suffered damage from trace amounts of antimatter. The repulser is hopefully a way to shield us from interstellar nano-meteorites."

"That sounds like something we could have used. You have a way to identify which star systems are antimatter?"

"Yes, there is a minor offset in one of the hydrogen spectral bands. There is another method; touch it and see if you explode."

Captain Cheasobod said, "We accidentally tried that. We haven't had good luck with that method."

I said, "And that makes a good setup for the main item for this meeting."

"Are you agreeable to providing us assistance, contacting our people, and returning us home?"

"No, we have one more pressing item we need to review before that. Trishah Maconda, go over what you found."

She said, "My name is Trishah Maconda. I am one of the Sulimon, part of the Federated Worlds. I ran a stress analysis on the damage to your ship, as well as spectral analysis and radioisotopic analysis. Your initial assumption was that the ship hit an antimatter micro-meteorite of a larger nano-meteorite. Luna, start the slide show."

The first image was a version of the Far-Singer in pristine condition.

"Now, the current state of the ship."

The image changed, showing the massive damage to the front end.

"Now, put up the model showing the expected damage from an antimatter meteorite."

The image changed slightly.

"Now rapidly flick between them."

The two destroyed images started flickering from one to the other and back.

"Now zoom in on the lateral strut identified in their database as K-17."

Captain Cheasobod and his wife stood up and walked over directly in front of the display.

"Shit, this wasn't a meteorite, it was a missile, and it contained an antimatter warhead."

Luna said, "We reached the same conclusion. This part of the damage would be riddled with small holes. It shows a ballistic penetration, followed by an explosion, not exploding on contact. If it did not directly strike the main keel strut, the detonation would have been deeper into the ship, and there would be no survivors."

I said, "Well, captain, this looks like a tactical weapon. Care to elaborate? Does your race happen to be engaged in a war we should know about?"

He sighed, "My race is a bunch of fracking idiots. Yes, we are herbivores, but we have evolved into a militaristic and aggressive race. There were several primary factions. The governments tried to keep the groups separate, and they even tried to have them work together, but it never quite worked out. There were three main factions, the 'Pullis' who wanted to stop space exploration and stay at home. The 'Marku' was the most ambitious about space exploration. Lastly, there was the 'Chabon' who spent way too much of the country's resources on building up the military. We were part of the Marku. The weapon and the damage it did sounds like the work of the Chabon."

I said, "We would like to send a very small probe, one equipped with FTL and stealth, and the radio-band communicators we copied from your ship. We will move to a safer location in deep space and complete the repulser grid. That should also destabilize any missiles fired at us. It may still hit, but it should be a glancing blow."

Captain Cheasobod said, "I had come to grips with this as a disaster from unknown natural sources. We lost almost one-quarter of the crew immediately, and the number had grown to half the crew in the following weeks. My first wife was one of them. Another compartment we lost was the nursery. The youngest of us were killed in the initial explosion. We have only two juveniles that survived. When we entered the stasis pods, five remained outside. We had insufficient operational stasis pods. The oldest and the most badly injured made way for the youngest and the healthiest."

"We have reserved part of deck five for your people. They can remain there if they wish. We need one or two to be assigned to work with our military and help us understand what we can expect to encounter and how to deal with it."

Jennifer Woods said, "They can deal with me and the scientists if it is easier for them."

Captain Cheasobod said, "I will talk to my crew and figure out who to assign to help you.   We have had ground-based conflicts before and even aerial bombardments.   This would be the first I have heard of actual Space Warfare."

I said, "My race has had its share of wars.   The fact that we have a viable coalition of different races is a bit of a shock to some of us."

Princess Domonis laughed, "I think he is talking about us. Technically, we are still at war with the Federated planets, but we are negotiating the treaties at this time."

Dariea Fenagol Resonon said, "My people were at war with the others until this year.   That war went on for over 2,300 years."

"How did you end the wars?"

Everyone pointed at me and said in unison, "Him."

"Huh?"

Dariea Fenagol Resonon said, "He found a way to trick our leader into single combat."

"And he won?"

"No, he lost, but we forfeited because we violated the rules of the battle."

Princess Domonis said, "His way of getting us to stop fighting was even more creative."

"What did he do?"

"He managed to get our queen, the supreme leader of all of our people, pregnant."

"But, you are different races?   How would that even be possible."

"He sacrificed a bit of his humanity.   He is technically a chimera now; he has DNA from both races.

Marnia-12 said, "I don't mind sharing him for a good cause, like ending wars."

"Are you sleeping with him as well?"

"I am his bonded, but he saved all of us, and all of us are very grateful.   Also, my species (Snicker) finds human males to be quite enjoyable."

"I think this meeting has drifted off track, and we are about ready to break up.   Captain Cheasobod, I leave it up to you to determine when the salvage operations should be ended.   You should also leave a recorder with any personal messages you want on the ship before we leave."

"We should be ready to leave by tomorrow.   Can you set the medical chambers to link together so we can all talk with the remaining crew who are still in the chambers?"

Luna said, "Yes, we can do that. We can provide a recorder that is compatible with several interfaces.   And we can include the translation data files as well."

The meeting broke up shortly after that.

THE PROBES

We wound up staying for one more day. They wanted all the surviving crew together for the recorded memorial video. When it was done, they took a piece of the hull and had it cut into small medallions, and then they could all wear one around their necks.

Before we left, Luna added six more repulsers, bringing the total up to forty-three. Production of the remaining ones continued.

Our ship produced three of the FTL-capable stealth probes. These were sent out in FTL, and they exited over three of the target stars at one-light day distance and above the plane that the planets were orbiting.

Then, they stealthily approached until they reached a distance of one-light hour and listened for any radio traffic.

The probe that was over the home planet showed zero radio traffic. The one over the two smaller worlds showed only minimal automated messaging.

We waited another day and then sent the probes over the supposedly inhabited planets.

One probe heading to the planet that was supposed to be the least populated was fired upon by what we assumed was an automated defensive system. That missile had a small antimatter warhead. That probe was destroyed.

The one that was sent to their homeworld failed to detect any power signatures on the planet.

Luna reported, "I detect life signs on two continents and emissions consistent with burning fossil fuels. I do not detect any cars, but I see what appears to be a steam engine on parallel iron tracks. No radio transmissions, no electric lights, I put the population at two million."

"At the time we left, the population was eleven billion. There were thousands of satellites and five large space stations.

"There are the remains of a large number of geosynchronous satellites; the only thing in low orbit is a massive debris cloud. It looks like they bombed themselves back into pre-industrial civilization. Do you want to go down and attempt to make contact?"

"No, I would like to ask that we be accepted as permanent crew on this ship. I don't think there is anything there for us at this time."

Luna said, "I have detected one large ship in orbit of the fifth planet. I will have the probe head there. It may have survivors in a stasis pod."

"I don't have high expectations. What happens after this? Where do we go?"

"We were sent out here to investigate what we assumed was the discharge of a weapon that destroyed a survey ship. What we found was several ships composed of antimatter. We were only successful in contacting and getting one of them to turn around. When we are done here, we will head back to our area. We have FTL-capable ships; even with FTL, reaching our home will take most of a month. There will probably be some other crisis that needs our attention."

"Why will they need you specifically?"

"This ship is sentient and quite capable of defending itself. However, there is always someone stronger. We met one race that was overly aggressive. They currently have limited technology, but if they recover some wrecks in their area, we will be in trouble."

"Can you destroy the wrecks?"

"Possibly, only it's not our territory. The race that controls that area is far more advanced than us, and they follow some unusual rules. We don't want to have them go against us."

Zenner Cheasobod snickered and said, "You can't just have your captain impregnate their leader?"

That had me snort, and I choked. "Luna, please put up a side-by-side comparison of me and Mo... The leader of the Meduala."

The image showed me completely naked compared to a completely naked image of Queen Mineta, not counting her snake hair. I was a good four inches taller than her.

"With clothes on."

The image flicked and now showed us full clothes.

"Now show a comparison, with clothes to an adult female Ogre."

The image changed and now showed my six-foot height compared to a she-Ogre beast that was eighteen feet high and was wearing several human-sized skulls on its belt and not much else.

"Okay, I retract my last suggestion. I may also need to change my uniform."

Luna said, "The ship-suits can protect against vacuum; a little spilled liquid will not damage them."

"You fought against one of those?"

"We fought against the equivalent of a pre-teen nerdy little girl version of that. She was only a little over double our size."

"How many of you did she kill?"

"One killed, one we managed to patch together, but we needed to regrow her arm and some internal organs. I only lost a few fingers on one hand."

"You have a weapon that can kill that thing?"

"We have multiple weapons that can do the job. Unfortunately, most are not hand-held. The ones that a human can lift are single shots, and they also do massive collateral damage."

The two Forandicates we were now working with were Zenner Cheasobod, the captain's niece, and Corporal Growler Kanaba. The latter seemed to annoy the former at any opportunity, which usually left Zenner Cheasobod in a perpetually bad mood.

Captain Cheasobod said, "You two need to watch your attitude. This isn't my ship, but I am sure I could find some used toothbrushes and have you clean deck five with them."

34

They glared at the other captain but finally said, "Yes sir," and returned to sitting quietly.

We redeployed the surviving two reconnaissance drones to the last two of the Forandicate's planets. One was actively having a massive war, and a rough approximation said they would deplete most of the planet's resources within two years. The other showed no signs of life, but an active orbital missile launcher destroyed the drove.

I said, "We are done here; how are we doing with the repulsers?"

"We have twelve more we can install, and the remaining twelve will be ready in a few days. I would rather add them and not need them than need them and have them sitting in storage."

"I say we remain here for two days and search for any survivors."

"Two days and sixteen hours, including installation time."

"Whatever, use the time to also make more of the stealth reconnaissance drones. It would be better if you could make them capable of exploring any derelict ships we find. I want a way they can operate an airlock. If they get taken out, we can build more. If we lose some marines, we all have a bad day."

SEARCHING DERELICTS

The new repulsers actually made the ship's front end look very impressive. Luna took the extra time and repaired all the antimatter damage. The ship now looked almost new.

The ship near the home planet was a lost cause. It had stasis pods, but the reactor was blown. It was a radioactive death cave, and the stasis pods were the type that needed external power.

The search continued, and three more ships were found. The first two were floating coffins. The third one had four operational stasis pods, and these were recovered entirely by the new remotes. We had them scanned thoroughly for explosives and contaminants before we allowed the shuttle containing them to dock.

"Bad news, It's a Chabon ship."

"Is the language the same?"

"No, they speak a different language. They refused to speak the same language as we did. Even their writing is different.

"If we leave it, is there any chance someone else will rescue them?"

"Who? Everyone else is dead or knocked back to a pre-industrial level of technology. I show less than one hundred years remaining on the stasis pod. Wait, these readings are all wrong."

"What do you show?"

"They have multiple occupants in several of them. One has three children, the other two have two children, and the last shows one adult, but she is pregnant."

"Extract them. What is the condition of the ship?"

"It appears to be a refugee ship, with lots of bodies, and most were quite young. Something failed, and they were unable to repair it. I am logging into their computer..... Negative, the computer has fried. I show it suffered a coolant leak, and the coolant flooded the processor room, resulting in massive electronic failures. The idiots

36

used some type of conductive coolant.   Everything shorted out. The reactor power is on manual control.   They wired it to eight stasis pods. Only four of them are still operational.   What do you think would be less disturbing to wake them up? The race they are paranoid about or complete aliens?"

"Maybe use the mechanical drones."

Luna said, transferring them to the medical pods.   The first one is open. I identify two juveniles, equivalent to ages fourteen or fifteen. Both are female.

.. .. ..

"The second one is now being opened. The occupant is a female, approximately age twenty. She is pregnant and looks like she is six or seven months pregnant. Their gestation period is ten months, so she has three or four months to go."

"The last one is…   Crap, it had three children in it. One is not viable.   The two survivors appear to be ages ten or maybe eleven. I am transferring them to the medical pods.   The last one… These pods were not meant to support multiple patients.   We are lucky two survived.   It looks like they reprogrammed the pods, but it failed to connect to the third patient's bloodstream correctly.   Two more surviving females, apparent ages thirteen or fourteen."

"How long do they need in the medical pods?"

"Four or five days, all had issues with exceeding the chamber capacities.   I was able to read nothing at all from the ship's computer."

I said, "Wait a minute, did you examine the other chamber occupants?"

"No, I am sending one of the drones back to read the information.   All are deceased; what are you looking for?"

"Ages and genders."

Fifteen minutes later, the scanning was complete.   Two contained older adult males, and the rest were overloaded with younger females."

"How old were the males?"

"All were over forty years old."

"I have a bad feeling; this seems like an underage harem, and the males were probably the cult leaders."

"I wish I could refute that hypothesis, but the males died because they took firearms into the chambers with them, and the weapons leached toxic chemicals when they broke down in the stasis fluid. They probably only lasted for a few years before failing."

"Captain Cheasobod, what do you think?"

He was visibly shaking, "Ask me in ten minutes. I am so angry at the moment I can't think straight."

"Does your race consume alcoholic beverages to become drunk?"

"Yes, but they didn't include any on our ships. If you have something, I will see if I can poison some of my livers with it. First Lieutenant Chisai Cheasobod, you have command of our motley group of refugees until I am sober again."

She approached her husband and said, "Since you are temporally relieved of command..." She then solidly punched him in the chin."

"Thanks, honey. I will return the favor after you get the bottle if there is any left."

Growler Kanaba said, "Sorry about this; this is probably why they never include alcohol on our ships."

"Half your crew dead, most of your race dead or reduced to pre-industrial. Getting drunk and punched doesn't seem too strange."

Acting Captain Cheasobod said, "I hope the kids are not abused and brainwashed."

We were ready to leave two hours later, and Jake Anderson had assumed temporary command.

Jake said, "Luna, do we have everything we want from the damn ship?"

"Yes."

"Put the external cameras on all the internal monitors. Are we at a safe distance?"

"We are at five miles. The engines are set to do a hard reverse as soon as we fire."

"Use both barrels; this range should have the shotgun shells spread to cover most of the derelict. Fire when ready."

BOOM!!

The ship immediately started a hard reverse, and you could feel the compensators fighting the G-forces.

The ship counted down the thirteen seconds it took for the hail of BBs to reach the derelict.

"A hit, it didn't explode, but the damage is still extensive."

Private Cheasobod said, "What did that weapon do?"

"It perforated most of this side of the ship with small holes. It's not the most efficient weapon, but no one will ever want to enter that ship. It is filled with shrapnel and …"

Luna said, "A bit delayed, but it finally exploded."

"Never mind, it's now destroyed."

Three days later, the repulser was finally at the complete configuration of sixty-one gravity repulsers, and the ship was tweaking the fields to get the best effect.

"We are ready to depart. The children and the females have successfully learned the common tongue language. They need to stay in the medical pods for a few more days, but we can talk to the older female now while she is still in the medical pod."

"Connect her now. Audio only to start."

"Wa-Where am I? Wait? What? What is this strange language that I find myself speaking?"

"You were rescued from the derelict ship. Can you explain what happened?"

"I ah.. I am Kenadi Minga. Err, I gladly will serve my master, Mr. Chang, and the others."

"The males did not survive; only you, the child in your belly, and six female children survived."

"No, I am a loyal servant of Mr. Chang; please do not test me. I am loyal."

"Put the video on."

The image that came to her display was the conference room. We had the room filled with as many alien races as possible. We did not have any of the Forandicate in the room.

"800 years have passed since you went into the stasis chamber. Your race has managed to blow itself back into a pre-industrial state or kill itself off on the colony worlds."

"What are you?"

"We are an affiliated collection of races called the Federated Worlds."

"You are aliens, real aliens; your germs will kill us, alien germs."

"No, you have all been put in medical chambers. You are still in one. That has healed many of the things the stasis chambers messed up over the last 800 years."

"I am free of him. We are really free of them?"

"You and six female children are all that have survived. From a different ship, we have rescued some others; they are what I believe you call the Marku. Is that a problem?"

"I have never met any. Are we completely isolated? They are supposed to be incredibly warlike and violent."

"The ones I have met seem fine."

"What planet are we on?"

"We are on my ship."

"But I feel gravity. Are we under constant acceleration?"

"No, this ship uses artificial gravity."

"Aliens, ships with artificial gravity, non-aggressive Marku, what else could happen?"

"We are about to accelerate to far faster than the speed of light and head to a different part of the galaxy, the home for one of our alien races."

"How long do I need to stay in this prison chamber?"

"It is a medical pod, and it is repairing centuries of damage. The child you are carrying is doing well."

"It is the son of that vile madman. I care not what you do with the monsters spawn inside of me. I will reject it as soon as it leaves my body. I will smash it ….. She started crying at that point."

Then she just dropped unconscious.

Luna said, "I put her out; we can postpone dealing with this problem for now."

"Head for home; hopefully, the return trip will be uneventful."

I spoke too soon…

A NEW PROBLEM

The new repulsers were power cycled and calibrated for fifteen minutes in normal space, and then we entered FTL and started for home. The calibration procedure continued. The current draw was much higher than the ship was originally intended to support. Still, it worked for almost three hours before the electrical power cables to the repulsers melted one section, and it welded itself to the hull. We dropped out of FTL.

"What happened?"

"Unknown, the current draw was within the expected range when operated in normal space. In FTL, it was 35% higher than expected. I was running a phase-shifting calibration, so I assumed it was acceptable. The power cable was rated at 200% of the expected load. It was still below the expected limit."

Jennifer Woods said, "I was monitoring the test. The numbers just don't add up. Luna, put the current flow diagrams twenty-seven through thirty on display."

The screen showed the images, but it didn't make a lot of sense to me.

"Then I noticed the discrepancy. How can the current be higher in the cable to the repulsers than it is exiting the reactor?"

"They shouldn't be. The force profile of the vortex effect is also much higher than expected. That makes it more effective and the ship safer from stray antimatter or any normal meteorites."

"So the side effects are beneficial, but the power is way too high. I recommend you reduce the power and increase the rating on the power cable. The one thing that worries me is the power out of the reactor. Melting a cable is one thing; overloading the reactor is a much more concerning issue."

"Are the repairs safe to do in FTL?"

"Normally, I would say yes, but I would rather play it safe… We have moved close to sixteen light years, and the closest stars are all normal matter."

"Do a deep scan while we wait. How long will it take to replace the power cable?"

"Twelve hours if I increase the rating by 30%, twenty-four hours if I increase their rating by 50%."

"Anderson, any emergencies at home? Do we need to shave half a day off the arrival time?"

Luna said, "There were none."

"You saying that out loud just increased the odds of a panic situation on Earth by 200%."

"Do the full 50% increase and also add more insulation. Let me know if the scans detect a grain of sand."

Two hours later, Luna reported, "Captain, the scans have detected a small debris field, but no ship."

Jennifer said, "We are on it; permission to FTL hop closer to evaluate it?"

"Negative, head there using the sub-light drive, and don't push them past nominal levels. We have almost a day to sit here. We are what? One light-hour away?"

"Fifty-seven light-minutes. Using the sub-light-engines, we can reach it in twenty hours. Do we still have any of the probes? You can have one of them hop in FTL and evaluate it."

"Probe launched, entering FTL in 3, 2, 1, FTL, done, Scanning the debris field."

"Matter or antimatter?"

"Normal matter. Materials consistent with an FTL capable ship hull, but much higher in aluminum than expected. I detect a faint ion trail leading away from the debris cloud. I would guess they had an accident and then limped off after repairs. The path is directly towards a small red dwarf Star. They probably needed to make repairs.   Conventional sub-light could take them anywhere between fifty and several hundred years to reach the star.   We don't know how fast their sub-light engines are. I hope they have stasis pods."

"Are there any biological signatures in the debris?"

"No bodies, and nothing that the scanners have detected."

"If we have the probe do some short FTL hops, can we estimate their speed and position?"

We should have numbers after three or four hops. Are we back to the old staple of rescuing people from derelicts?"

"It's the one task I usually feel good about after."

Princess Domonis started laughing.   Then she said, "You seem to enjoy ending some wars too."

That got chuckles from everyone.

"Can we get enough data from the remote probe to determine the approximate location of the mystery ship?"

"Not with the current probe.   I could start printing the parts for one large enough to do the job.   It would be slightly larger than one of the shuttles, with no life support, just a honking big sensor grid. It will take twenty-one days to complete."

"Set that as a background task.   We may need one later.   Do we have room in the shuttle bay?"

"No need; it can easily fit in the doghouse."

Anderson said, "We have a doghouse?"

"It stores the maintenance drones.   It also is where the parts were assembled for the repulser grid array."

"Can we store weapons there as well?"

"Yes, but that is one of the reasons I neglected to mention it earlier.   It doesn't have easy access by biologicals, and I didn't want you filling all my ports with weapons."

I said, "Luna, please give Anderson all the specifications. Anderson, review the specifications but don't assume you have free run to fill every square meter of space with WMDs. We need to stay on the good side of the Ghost Ships. They have restrictions about harming their creators; however, they don't have any similar restrictions against harming us. It would be way too easy for them to disable our ship."

Doctor Cora Smith said, "Can I review that data with you, Major Anderson?"

"Keep Jennifer Woods in that loop, too. We should probably include some others, Trishah Maconda…   Anyone else?"

That discussion then got sidelined.

Luna said, "I am sending the small probe out; I doubt it will detect anything."

Jennifer Woods said, "How about sending another of the small probes to the red dwarf? It won't detect a residual gas trace but may detect the ship if it is in orbit around a moon."

"That sounds reasonable.   Make it so."

.. .. ..

The replacement of the power cabling went normally.   When it was done, Luna reported, "We were ready to enter FTL.   Where are we going?"

"Any sign of the missing ship at the red dwarf star?"

"Nope."

"Do the trick you mentioned earlier, take three hops along the course, and see if you can compute the speed and position."

"FTL in 3, 2, 1, Now"

Thirty seconds later.   "Exiting FTL now."

We waited a few minutes.

"Well?"

"No sign of the ship, backtracking to the halfway mark, FTL in 3, 2, 1, Now."

"Exiting FTL."

"I see the vapor trail. It has not expanded much at all. I think the accident was a lot more recent than I originally estimated. Starting long-range scan."

After twenty minutes, we were getting bored, "Find anything?"

"No, I will do some micro-FTL jumps in rapid succession."

She didn't have to say when she was doing them; my stomach did a flip-flop about once every ten seconds.

After a few minutes, she reported, "Found them, one more hop, and we will be at one-light second."

The last hop was completed normally.

"What do we have?"

"I am holding back until we know more. It's not a ship design we are familiar with. I have summoned Captain Cheasobod to look at it. I would summon the pregnant female, but we neglected to ask her name, and she must stay in the medical pod for a few more hours. What do we do about the child she is carrying?"

"We can discuss that later. Given how she feels about the father, she will likely reject caring for it."

"Captain Cheasobod will be here in a few minutes. Someone was showing him and his crew the game Room."

A minute later, we heard them approaching. Sophia Nikolaou was with them. They were discussing some video game strategy."

"Captain Robinson, what can I do for you?"

Luna put the ship image on the screen.

"We found a damaged ship that was FTL capable. Now, it is running at sub-light. Do you recognize the design?"

"No, however, we did not have FTL in my time. We don't know exactly when the war was fought."

Luna said, "Probably within twenty years of when you entered the stasis pods. If your people developed FTL, or the other factions did, it wasn't on any of the ships we have seen."

We stared at the image for a few minutes. "A nice design, but not in the style of any of the factions."

I said, "Send out the usual array of hello messages. See if they respond to anything. What is the ship's current status?"

"They accelerated to 0.022 of light speed and have been coasting at that speed for several months, maybe years. Whatever the damage is, I can't see any outward damage at this range. I see what is probably a power signature and something unidentified, possibly a weapon."

"Let's try all the radio links we have and wait an hour before we get any closer. Let me know if anything changes. Keep ready to hop into FTL if it looks like it is charging weapons. Sound the level-1 caution/alert and announce to the crew that they should stow any loose objects."

After a few minutes, Luna said, "We have an automated response. My best guess is we are badly formatting the messages, and it's asking us what we are trying to say."

A few minutes later, "Data connection established, learning to say hello. Very, very slowly learning to say hello."

After about ten minutes of minimal progress, Luna said, "Minor power surge, consistent with waking someone from stasis. They have a dumb computer, and it finally decided to ask for directions."

Nothing happened for a bit, and then an active radar ping came out, followed by many more. Eventually, some generic commands started showing up.

"Ah, they finally enabled an AI. They must lock it down to just a simple computer when in stasis. Learning their alphabet and basic syntax. This will take a while."

Two hours later, we were still only communicating between the AIs.

"They just triggered more of the stasis chambers to wake up. They have started enabling a video channel, but it is just a calibration pattern so far. It's cycling through various audio formats. Time for everyone to assume their last supper poses and all bunch together on one side of the conference table."

Another thirty seconds, and then the video was enabled.

I wasn't sure what the thing on the screen was at first. If the video was correct, it was like an octopus was using a snail's shell as a home. The voice came out translated into standard trade talk language.

"Greetings, I am Snargelet-Po of the Yel-Brike. Please identify yourselves."

"Hello, I am Keith Robinson, species Human, part of a Federation of Different worlds. We noticed that your ship appears to have a problem. Do you need assistance?"

We waited, and the translation was slower than usual.

"We have suffered mechanical problems. Your ship is massive. Can you spare 0.07-creds of palladium and 5-creds of tungsten?"

Luna said, "Working on the translation, I believe they want 4.3 pounds of palladium and 310 pounds of tungsten. That amount of tungsten is trivial from my spare stores. The palladium would be 19% of my spares."

Anderson said, "I am all right with the requested transfer amounts. We will still have sufficient reserves for an emergency."

Luna said, "The quantities are consistent with repairing an older style FTL centrifuge multiplier. We can have the material ready in half an hour and use a transfer drone to deliver it."

"Okay, let them know." Half an hour later, we sent the drone over.

"They are offering us something as a trade item, but the translator has not yet completely explained what it is."

Anderson said, "Keep whatever it is in the dog house and treat it like plutonium until we know what it is."

"Accept the offered item, but scan the crap out of it. Good plan."

Twenty minutes later, "They thank us for the supplies. They can make the repairs themselves now. It sounds like the item they gave us is a communication device. It looks like an oval-shaped hand mirror, about six inches tall and four inches wide. It is extremely thin. About the thickness of three sheets of paper."

Anderson said, "Is it powered?"

"Yes, the frame is powering it. One side is reflective, the other shows... It's a video communications device. I think it is the being we spoke to earlier."

"Let them know that we will be presenting the device to someone on our home planet later for evaluation."

When we disconnected, Princess Domonis said, "You didn't do your usual introduce everyone going around the table."

"No, and I thought I did good not running away screaming. That thing was a fricking Lovecraftian horror."

Luna said, "I detected conversations on an open microphone on the bridge of their ship. They thought about the same thing about us. We were disgusting monsters to them as well. Even your hair, your nest of huge snakes, was disgusting to them."

"My hair is beautiful!"

"Only to another Meduala."

Marnia-12 said, "I didn't find it ugly. It looked delicious. I remember the meal at the restaurant with all the ocean animals in the giant tanks. What was the one that was cut up into rings?"

"That was calamari, and that thing did look a bit like a squid. Luna, you can keep the communicator. Is it quantum-based so that it will work over long distances?"

"Yes."

"You can chat all you want with the Calamari. Find out what they are doing in our area, and let them know how to use Q-Band to say hello if they run into any other ships."

Anderson said, "Are we done here? Can we get back into FTL and head home?"

The answer was yes. We started home again...

MORE PROBLEMS

The other Forandicate and the children were ready to wake up in two days.

She awoke from the medical pod and looked up to see herself surrounded by different monsters.

"Good morning, Captain. I see that the visions I assumed I had were not just dreams. Is it true the vile beast is dead?"

"There were two older males in failed stasis chambers. None survived. The children are ready to wake up, but we wanted to get you stabilized first."

"Where are we? What happened?"

"Captain Cheasobod, can you explain that?"

"Hello miss, I am Captain Cheasobod, formerly of the ship the Far-Singer. We were a Marku ship, and our ship was destroyed by a weapon we were not familiar with. This collection of different species rescued us in a massive ship.

"I am Kenadi Minga, and unfortunately, I am part of the Chabon. I carry the offspring of Lord Zenatol, and I do not wish to carry this abomination for another minute. Can you please rip this out of me before it grows anymore?"

"We don't usually support killing a late-term healthy unborn fetus without medical reasons. There are usually some other options."

Captain Cheasobod said, "Oh, I am familiar with the evil of Lord Zenatol. I hate even to suggest terminating a life that early, but the father of this child is, or was, evil incarnate.

Marnia-12 said, "We should be able to have the unborn child transferred to an artificial womb on the ship. We have several. That way, she will be free from the temptation to damage herself and the unborn child."

"That is a temporary solution; the child still has the genetics of he that is the root of evil."

51

Luna said, "There is a possibility; captain, you are the clue. The captain is actually a chimera. He contains the genetics of several species. He has fathered a child that will grow up to be a Meduala royal."

"I don't get what you are suggesting?"

"After the child is transferred into an artificial womb, I could then replace most of its genetic signature with that of another."

"You would sample a different Forandicate and convert the unborn child to the other genetic data?"

"We have viable DNA from the third child that did not survive in the stasis chamber. The child would then retain minimal genetics from the father or the mother."

"That is acceptable. What else remains from the ship we were on?"

"Nothing. We used it as target practice. No one will ever salvage nothing from it."

"What of my people?"

Captain Cheasobod said, "Our homeworld has fought a terrible war, and from what I saw, what remains were reduced to a primitive level and are now struggling to survive. The secondary worlds were even in worse shape."

"We are leaving them to their fate?"

"About a dozen of us now live between your group and our survivors; more than half are children."

I said, "We are returning to our worlds. We can send a ship out in a few years and drop you off on your world. Now, you are simply refugees. In a few years, you can be teachers and try and help your people. I ask you, If you had a ship and returned now, what would happen?"

"It depends on where we land. I can see the most likely outcome: if I lived, all three of my eyes would be gouged out, and I would be a slave, and they would take the ship."

"I hate to say this, but you don't sound that far removed from a slave now."

"I was a prize, taken by force, that played along so that I would live. I was originally raised as minor nobility, and then I watched my parents be fed alive to a monokaka. My sister would have been fed to them next if I had not agreed to be the beast's concubine. Speaking of my sister, can you show me the faces of the others you saved? I hope and pray she is among them."

The four children's faces were shown, and it was not one of them. Then, the face of the one who died was shown, and that was her.

"I agree to your replacing the genetics of the bastard I carry with my sister's genetics. Please put me out and do this. I need this removed, and I want my sister's essence back, even if her spirit has left."

We let her go back to sleep.

A few hours later, she was in a medical pod that was connected to an artificial womb, and the unborn child was extracted.

"How will this genetic overlay modification work?"

"The child will be put in a torpor state, similar to a bear hibernating, and then the modified genetic material will replace much of the existing material. The child is at six months of development. The following month will revert the child to about five months of development, and then she will grow up normally."

"How much of her genetic material will be replaced?"

"She will be 97.5% the sister and 2.5% the child of the evil asshole."

"Can you make it closer to 100% the sister?"

"That will take… Yes, it can be done; the sister's clone will be re-born in ten months. The child will then be 99.9% the sister."

"Do it."

Anderson said, "How do you get it close to 100%?"

I said, "You probably don't want to know the details."

Luna said, "He is correct; you don't want to know the details."

"The sister will be effectively reborn?"

"A clone of the sister will be reborn.   She will have almost none of the original fetus's DNA."

"And what of the current unborn child?"

"To get an almost complete genetic replacement, the genetic replacement will be run for three months.   The resulting child will then have been reverted back to the equivalent of three months of gestation.   The child will be reduced to only a scaffolding and then completely regrown.   It remains technically alive during the entire process."

"That almost sounds like killing the child and then replacing it."

"If you could go back in time to 1889 and erase Adolph Hitler in his mother's womb and replace him with Anne Frank, would you do it?"

"That would completely change history. That is not a valid analogy."

"Maybe it is. Future history will be unchanged in this case. We are replacing the child of a monster with someone who suffered at the hands of the monster.   The unborn child with the cursed DNA would forever have a dark shadow hanging over it. We are simply removing the shadow."

"Yeah, I think you were right. I really didn't want to know..."

Luna said, "I am summoning the rest of the command crew to the conference room.   The biological technicians and the drone can handle the rest.   You have a priority call from Earth."

BIG PROBLEMS

The usual command crew all showed up in the conference room, including Princess Domonis.

Anderson said, "You know, you are technically not part of the command crew?"

"I take my role as observer very seriously." The silly grin she couldn't suppress indicated differently.

When the last of us were sitting, Luna put the screen up. It was General McFarland of the Space Force.

Anderson said, "What can we do for you, General?"

"Not much of anything with you stuck out where you are. I am asking you to prioritize returning as fast as possible over stopping and rescuing any more survivors. We are sending you the coordinates of where to dock. It is close to a Sulimon orbital shipyard. I have been asked to get a verbal guarantee from Princess Domonis that she will ignore the location of the shipyard and not report it to anyone associated with the Meduala. The treaty has not been officially ratified yet. It is in the works, but the papers have not been signed."

She got an evil grin on her face. "I could be persuaded to ignore just about everything else on the trip back if a tiny little favor was granted. One that is guaranteed to take my mind off of everything else."

I groaned.

Marnia-12 started laughing.

Jennifer Woods said, "They are pimping you out again? Do Cora and I need to start retaking your blood and tissue samples regularly again?"

Princess Domonis said, "When do we get to your not-so-secret base? How many days?"

"(Sigh), You will be there in fifteen days."

"That works. If I take the trigger hormones starting tonight, I should be in the correct cycle when we get there, and if you do your job right, I won't think about anything else."

"General, just what are we heading back for?"

"The big problem, the one Doctor Cora Smith had a problem with in the desert. We need to make some additions to your ship so you can fight that oversized problem."

"Oh, frigging hell."

Princess Domonis said, "Sorry, I accidentally picked up some visuals. I wasn't intentionally eavesdropping. That was frigging terrifying."

The general said, "What you probably saw was the equivalent of a teenage little girl version of one of these beings. The adults are much worse. Think of that as someone four or five years younger than Sophia Nikolaou."

"Crap. Do you want me to call Mother and see if she can provide any weapons?"

The General said, "I hope we don't need any more special weapons from any of the groups. The one weapon we are picking up is obsolete, but scientists think it may work for the particular creatures."

Princess Domonis said, "I think I will head to the game room. I need to get my mind off of the image I saw. I saw another image, and that was Cora Smith lying in a pool of... Urrp, excuse me, I think I am gonna be..."

She ran for the bathroom across the hall... She didn't make it in time.

Luna said, "The clean-up drones are on their way. I suspect the royals rarely ever personally see graphic violence."

"I think we can continue with this. What is the new weapon?"

The general said, "A piece of nasty hand-held anti-ship weaponry. It was intended to make a shuttle incapable of reaching space by putting a large hole in the side. Too large for a standard patch. It looks a lot like a bazooka. No recoil, as the back is open, but you don't want to stand behind it. It fires a 4.5-inch wide section of pipe. Behind that is a detachable propulsive rocket. It puts a hole almost five inches wide in a lightly armored shuttle hull. It should be effective against an armored Ogre."

Dariea Fenagol Resonon said, "They tend to fight using a well-structured combat. They also prefer swords as their weapon of choice. Part of me thinks this weapon you have described is barbaric and violates all the protocols of civilized war. That said, I would instantly shoot the fracking monster with one as soon as I saw it. I saw the aftermath of the little girl Ogre and the soldier, or what was left of him. I would much rather be known as live savage than remembered as a cultured splatter stain on the wall."

Whatever we did, it was going to be a long wait; we had a little over two weeks of FTL travel ahead of us.

.. .. ..

Fifteen days later…

We were a few hours away from the destination when we got a call from Headquarters. We assembled the usual crew in the conference room. This unexpectedly included Princess Domonis.

"Why are you here for this meeting?"

General McFarland said, "We asked for her."

The screen then split, and the Meduala queen appeared on a different display.

She said, "Congratulations, you have officially ended another war. We have agreed to a negotiated peace settlement. We also have a ship that will meet you at the unnamed not-so-secret base. There, you will pick up someone who can probably help in the fight against the Ogres. Someone that Domonis is familiar with but has never actually met. She is a bit of a strange being."

"Princess Domonis, by my orders, you are to serve as the host for Kelapaton. This decree is absolute. Do you understand?"

She had instantly gone white; all the color had drained from her face. She was visibly shaking. "Yes, Mother, I hear, and I shall obey."

"Good, that is settled. She will probably be unhappy with this suggestion, but it is necessary for our continued survival. We need to prevent these Ogres from ever gaining FTL travel. Treat her as you would any dangerous weapon. We will return Kelapaton to a different host when this is done. So fear not; you will be free of her eventually."

I said, "What is this thing she will 'host,' and what exactly do you mean by host?"

Princess Domonis said, "Am I allowed to speak freely about her?"

Queen Mineta said, "Yes, but only to the beings in the conference room, and they are not to speak of it unless directed by myself or the General."

Domonis said, "As you wish, Kelapaton was a Meduala royal who developed a unique ability. She can inhabit the body of another Meduala, and using that technique, she is, by far, the oldest entity known to any of us. Her ability has never been seen in any other Meduala since then. Inserting her presence requires pushing aside much of the host's persona. She has not inhabited a Meduala royal in many centuries, since the early days of the long war. She normally occupies a host that is selected, well... By the criminal courts. If the host she resides in is a convicted criminal, then there is no restriction on her taking over full control of the host. In that case, the host usually doesn't fully recover even after Kelapaton eventually leaves."

"I assume there is some reason to allow this mind leech to continue hopping from host to host?"

Queen Mineta said, "Yes, she has a second ability. She is effectively a weapon, and she has agreed only to take control of half of your mind. Her ability exceeds mine for that one specific function. I have the ability to bend steel and distort gravity. Her ability is more focused and perhaps more suited for fighting an Ogre.

On the downside, she is rendered almost helpless for close to an hour after using it."

Luna announced, "The ship will exit FTL in eight minutes. I detect transponders of two ships in the designated area. One mid-sized freighter and one small shuttle; the shuttle is unusually well-armored. The instructions are to have the freighter dock on one of the external ports, and the shuttle will be received in the landing bay. Captain, you are requested in the landing bay."

The video conference shut down at this point.

Domonis asked, "Captain, before we go, I have a request. Can I have a few moments alone with you?"

Everyone else was leaving, so I said, "Sure, I guess so."

We waited until everyone had left and the door closed.

"Please, Allow me a slight transgression, something to remember and dream about."

"I guess so..."

She leaped onto me and started kissing and hugging me. Then I felt the sharp pain of multiple fangs from her snake hair sinking into me.

She squeezed me tight, "I only had a few dozen bit you. I want to sense you, and the markers will let me." She continued hugging me. "I am terrified of her; I wish we could have had more, perhaps someday, when this is over. Then It will be time for us."

Then she bit my ear and started sucking on it."

"Are you drinking my blood?"

"Humm, homm."

"I think we need to go."

She just clung to me. She was still sucking on my ear.

Finally, she released me and said, "I am ready." I noticed she was crying.

We headed out and eventually joined the others outside the shuttle docking bay.

Lune announced, "Exiting FTL in 3, 2, 1 exiting."

As usual, the only discernible effect was a minor wobble effect in the gravity. Like being on an elevator and then stopping rapidly when reaching the floor.

Luna said, "The cargo freighter is now approaching for docking, and the shuttle is approaching."

Marnia-12 said, "What? Keith, you are bleeding from the ear, and you have a few dozen puncture wounds. There wasn't enough time, even for a quickie; what were you two doing?"

Doctor Cora Smith pulled out a kit she always had at her side, like a fanny pack, and said, "Give me your arm." She did a few quick alcohol wipes and took a blood sample while I stood there.

"You are probably fine, but we do need to keep track of what new crap you get injected with. If you feel faint, you are going into the closest medical pod, which is one room over. You will need to hop in a medical pod later, as that can test other things. Oh, she actually looks a lot worse than you; I assume that is jitters about what will be on the shuttle?"

"Yeah, you could say that."

Luna said, "They are both docking now."

"I thought it would be a fancy shuttle. This one looks beat up. Heavily armored but beat up and in need of a new paint job."

Luna said, "The designation is "Prisoner Transport. I don't think they care about the paint."

Some medical technician I had seen before but couldn't remember her name showed up at that point and handed Princess Domonis a blue pill and a glass of water.

"Yeah, this is probably a good idea," she swallowed the pill. "Ha, I actually took one of these voluntarily; that sure is different."

After the shuttle landed, the outer chamber door closed, and the shuttle bay started pressurizing.

"The cargo shuttle is docked, and they are unloading crates of weapons. That will take a while."

When the shuttle bay was under pressure, the door opened and out walked an older Meduala female with normal-length tendrils and a scar over one eye.

She said, "Let's get this done; this host is fighting. She hated having me in her, and now she doesn't want me to leave. Oh, you are a pretty one. Are you my new host…"

She jumped in front of me and started sniffing.

"Holy fraggile crap, the rumors are true. What is it they call your race? Humans, but so much more. You smell… Delicious…"

I said, "And you smell like you haven't bathed in months."

"Hmm, probably only five weeks, six at the most. The new host is so nice and clean. A minor royal?"

Princess Domonis said, "Major royal, second level G, and fourth level bender. I am also closely watched by Mother."

"Yes, I have met her several times. Once, when she was only a child, the last time was when this host was presented to me. Let's get this over with. I will be the rider, and you will be fully aware."

The new Meduala stood still, and Princess Domonis walked over and stood directly in front of her; then, she took a deep breath, leaned in, and touched her forehead to the new Meduala. They stayed like that for a few minutes and then separated. Then the new Meduala fell to her knees and started mumbling, "I am free, it's gone, I am finally free."

Then, two new meduala came out of the shuttle wearing military uniforms.

"Prisoner QB7532902, you will be remanded to the maximum security prison at Tellos and will spend the remainder of your life there."

"Yes, I am free, take me away, free... free..."

They led her away.

Princess Domonis said, "She is in here with me; she is crawling over my thoughts, my mind..."

Then, in a slightly deeper voice, she said, "I am Kelapaton. I will try and speak using this changed voice so you can tell us apart. I will now surrender the voice and learn this body...."

She jumped back. She looked at me. "You have seeded a child with Mother and with Menanaka? And you still live!"

Marnia-12 patted her swollen belly and said, "And the one in here as well."

"That's... Impossible."

"That's me, the impossible guy. I don't know what your ability even is. Supposedly, it may be useful for us against the Ogres. Those are the bad aliens. We are not sure we will even meet any of them. We have other weapons that should prove effective. We have only killed one, and it was a small one, only twelve feet tall; the adults are eighteen or possibly more."

"I was given a training session for your language, and that included measurement units.... What the? Your minds are fading. A fricking royal is somehow becoming a fracking Null! What did you do?"

About two minutes later, Princess Domonis said, "I seem to be back to myself, or myself as a Null. This is good; give the mind leech time to contemplate nothing. I can still sense it. She is screaming, but no one is listening. I like this."

Luna said, "The cargo freighter is almost unloaded. They also unloaded a team of four Sulimon military that is trained on the obsolete weapon. They were part of a contingency group. They trained different groups on just about every possible weapon. Think of it as if a Seal Team was trained on crossbows for a special assignment."

"Yeah, I could see that. They would be quieter and have no thermal signature after firing like a gun. I could see them also possibly training with swords."

Luna said, "Given the one battle with an Ogre, yes, and oversized battle axes as well. They will be using some of deck one, where the Pargaina were. The second floor has already been reclaimed after they left, but we are keeping it as a trauma center and moving most of the medical pods to deck two."

"How much did they unload?"

"Two hundred of the single-use ones that can be used in a vacuum. Then, there are some five-shot versions that they cobbled together. Those need a tripod and take a two-person crew to operate."

The shuttle was back in a vacuum, and the bay door opened and lifted off.

"I guess we are done here. Let's head back to the conference room and find out where we go next."

THE FORBIDDEN DESTINATION

Luna said, "I have received a destination; it was sent to us from the Ghost Ship BB7-QR-19. The destination was listed as in the 'Forbidden Zone,' Nothing off-putting about naming a space sector something like that."

"Who contacted who?"

"The ghost ships contacted the Earth. They had earlier requested me to provide them a link to our primary Ghost Ship Contact. That was BB7-QR-19. The Ghost Ships don't think the criteria to 'Bomb the Creators, what we call Ogres back to the stone age" had been met yet. They don't have any less extreme methods. They have agreed to let us attempt to destroy an FTL-capable derelict ship, and they are providing us with transportation to the location. We are not allowed to bomb it from orbit. We have to do it the old-fashioned way, with boots on the ground. Also, I am not allowed to go anywhere near the place. The Ghost Ships will provide you with a new ship. It is too large to fit in the Shuttle bay but can dock externally. It is not an AI ship. The good news is that the Earth gets a new ship when we are done."

"That sounds good for Earth but not necessarily for us. What type of ship is the one they are providing us?"

"It is a heavily modified derelict former ore freighter. It has room originally for bulk ore storage, now converted for additional crew berthing. So, it's not exactly luxury accommodations. It has no significant weapons, but they said we can add two A-10 Gatling guns, one on the front and one on the back. The most unusual thing about this class of ship is that the FTL drive is detachable. You will be delivered via FTL to outside of the star's gas giants, and then the FTL will detach and exit. It only returns after you succeed."

I said, "Sounds like they really don't want any FTL ships where the Ogres can access them. Have the Ogres reached the derelict ship with FTL? What other ship or ships do the Ogres have?"

"The Ogres have at least two ships with some sub-light drive working on them. The stellar system they are in is a red dwarf, and it has six rocky planets and five gas giants. The FTL-capable crashed ship is an old Meduala scout. It's on the larger moon of the second gas giant. The moon is huge, larger than Mars. It has a thin atmosphere of almost entirely carbon dioxide. It has evolved some plants but no advanced animals, or none they know of."

"Any chance there are survivors on the crashed ship?"

"Extremely unlikely. The ship crashed 1,000 years before the 2,000-Year War, so if anyone is in a stasis pod, it is at the extreme limits of survivability. Even those from the start of the war were running low or out of chemicals, and the batteries were never rated that long."

"Hey Domonis? Are you still driving? What is the other doing?"

"Kelapaton is pissed, but she can't do much. But she hears everything that I hear."

I said, "Luna, put the video on that shows the astronaut Ogre and superimpose an image of Domonis for size comparison."

The image appeared on the wall screen.

Domonis said, "Yeah, she sees that. I don't think she likes it."

"I don't like it either. Have all the available military, all those skilled at larger weapons outfitted with hardened spacesuits, and have the four Sulimon start training everyone on how to use the new weapon. Will the wall in the gunnery range survive live-firing these?"

"Yes, but we have a limited supply. They use some materials my replicators can't produce."

"Are you lacking some raw materials?"

"No, explosives are extremely dangerous to make with a conventional replicator. Same thing with electronics. I do have a specialized printer that makes the electronic assemblies. Then, it feeds completed assemblies to the bulk material and assembler printers. Explosive compounds need a very special printer. They usually produce the propellant separately, using more conventional chemical processes, and the shell casings are done in an intermediate-state assembly machine. Earth produces shells a lot more efficiently than I can.   However, I can produce spacesuits a lot faster than they can."

"So we have only 100 of the handheld units, and that is it?"

"Unfortunately, they are also only for one-time use.   A reusable version would weigh more than one man could easily operate.   Even the five-shot version is scrapped after the fifth shot."

"Assuming we can reach the ship, then how do we destroy the ship?"

Princess Domonis said, "Oh, I can do that, even without my cranial hitchhiker. Two things need to be destroyed: the computer, which is almost certainly not an AI, and the actual FTL drive.   I can crush them into metallic putty with my mind and mash them up. But not when I am in this null state."

Luna said, "The effect will wear off between twelve and twenty-four hours.   We can also give you the other pill if needed."

"Who is going?'

"Five Sulimons, Three Marines, Three of your Ninja girls, First Lieutenant Lilly Suzuki; this is Keijko Okada. and this is Tomoe Ishida.   Captain Anderson and Domonis/Kelapaton."

"And me."

"We would much rather you didn't."

"I would rather none of us had to go.   I assume the not-a-Ninja trio have some of their own toys?"

"The Marines will be using Mk 153 Shoulder-Launched Multipurpose Assault Weapons.   These are also sometimes called LARs.   The girls will probably be using the Sulimon's new weapon. It is a lot lighter and quieter than the Mk 153, as the hollow projectile is passive.   The Mk 153 is an anti-tank weapon. It's probably more effective but sure to draw a lot of return enemy fire.   They were associated with a branch of the Japanese military that doesn't officially exist. They were a group that operated in the shadows."

"Assassins?"

"I am sure some groups refer to the U.S. Seal Team-6 as those."

"What are they doing?"

"Two of them will stay on the ship, where they will remotely operate a stealth drone. Think of it as similar to the old VR-Goggles, only more immersive. The last one will be in a hard suit with adaptive camouflage. We have a location where we will land next to the ship. It is a two-and-a-half-day travel from here. As I said, Kelapaton will be fully recovered in twelve hours or less."

I said, "How are you doing Princess Domonis?"

"Kelapaton is still fully suppressed. I think I should report to medical and have your team check me over."

Jennifer Woods said, "Luna, page Doctor Cora Smith to the medical room B and have her meet us there. If you will excuse us, we need to at least document her condition."

When they left, Anderson said, "I wonder what she did to piss off the Queen so much that she got this shit assignment? I will have everyone with her from now on equipped with blue pill dart guns. I think we should also have one built into her hard suit, and I will link that via a dedicated quantum channel."

Luna said, "Not dedicated; I think multiple people need a way to command that option. I have searched the available databases on this Kelapaton, and she... It has been scrubbed from almost all records. The only thing I have found is that her hosts are always criminals and never for petty crimes."

I dismissed everyone and had First Lieutenant Lilly Suzuki stay behind. When it was just the two of us, I said, "Care to elaborate on exactly what your little group is?"

She smiled, "We were recruited as espionage agents. We are your security group. We specialize in non-standard weapons. Think of us as the Secret Service. We were assigned to jointly work with the U.S. forces two years ago, before all the space stuff. Unofficially, it was something to do with Zimbabwe. However, we were never officially involved in that."

"I remember watching that shit show on TV. They tried to blame that on everyone, but they never found anyone."

"They found some support people and tortured them, but all they ever got was that some exotic dancers had false IDs. They thought we were Chinese. It helps that we can fake lots of accents, and no one pays much attention to pretty girls."

"Are you safe from mind-readers? All the Meduala are mind readers, and now they put Kelapaton in the body of a royal, so I have no idea of her abilities."

"I don't know. They were supposed to do something to us to prevent mind reading, but none of us know what they did or if they actually did anything. The only one that knows is your AI, and she won't say."

Luna said, "That is locked down for all of our protection. Don't worry; protecting you and the crew is my highest priority."

.. .. ..

Kelapaton did not regain control of Princess Domonis's body for close to eighteen hours from when she took the pill.

She said, "I am not thrilled with this assignment, but it is better than being sitting in a maximum security prison and being to being implanted in thugs and criminals. The long war came and went, and they never needed my ability. But they kept me around, just in case. Now they have a threat so dangerous they have put me in a royal. She has contained me. I cannot leave her and enter another, and she has the ability to end us both. One of their precious royals. I used to be one; did they tell you that?"

"They haven't told us much about you. You are incredibly old and can hop from one mind to another. You are also a weapon; you have some ability that may be useful in fighting against these giants, these Ogres. In the last battle, it charged incredibly fast, cut one of us in half the long way, and then buried the axe more than an inch into a steel plate floor with one chop.   What do you do?"

"I am actually only about a day old.   The old me effectively dies during the transfer. However, the new one retains most of the memories.   I am now the 249th instance of me.   I keep track; there is not a lot else to do.   The longest I have been in a host was 57.5 years, and the shortest was two days.   Domonis, the new host, can easily bend steel with her mind.   I can also do that, but I can do something else: I can accelerate a large metallic mass with my mind. If Domonis crushed the FTL drive into a sufficiently tight ball, I could accelerate it like a rail gun and turn it into a bullet that can't be stopped.   Well, eventually, it will impact a star or a planet, and that will stop it."

"How fast can you accelerate a mass?"

"A standard starship can accelerate a mass of seventy-five of your pounds to 6,000 of your mph. To do that, it has to create a massive magnetic or electrostatic field.   I just mess with gravity.   I can accelerate a mass of 1,000 lbs to the speed of about 18,000 mph.   I can only do it once, and then I am wiped out for several hours.   It also needs to be very solid. If it is something like a shuttle, and it hasn't been compacted into a solid ball, I shatter it into a lot of small parts. That may not completely obliterate the FTL drive, computer, or other critical systems.   They chose us as a matched pair.   She crushes it, compacts it, and fuses it all together.   I then make it go away.

"You could use it as a weapon."

"Not effectively; my aim really sucks."

Luna said, "I show her historical accuracy with a 435-pound mass at 50% within twelve degrees and 90% within fifteen degrees. It also gets worse with a larger mass. At her maximum weight of 1,000 pounds, she is only at thirty degrees of accuracy. So she may be able to hit the broad side of a barn, but only if she was standing right next to one."

"What I said, my aim sucks with larger masses."

69

Then her voice changed back to Domonis, "If I have time to rip the derelict apart, the FTL drive and the old computer core should total just over 700 lbs. Mother wants both gone. I would have just gone after the FTL drive."

Luna said, "There is a chance the repair manual and specifications for the FTL drive will be on the computer. We need to make them both go away."

.. .. ..

"Captain, please report to medical room B. Kenadi Minga is now ready to exit her medical pod."

CAUSE AND EFFECT

"Kenadi Minga is about to wake up."

A few seconds later, Kenadi opened her eyes and saw that she was in a room filled with more of the strange two-eyed aliens.

The first thing she did was check her belly, and the bump was gone; her stomach was flat again.

"It is true, you have removed the spawn of the demon, and it is now growing in a different … Who is carrying what will be my sister?"

"Your real sister is dead. The clone will eventually look like her, but she will have entirely new memories. The process will take about ten months. That which was growing in you is no longer what it was. The replacement process will keep the child alive but reverses the growth cycle while replacing the genetics."

"That is fine; I would probably destroy what I was carrying if it came to full term. Assuming I was not self-destructive before that was completed. What of the others? The youths?"

"We are ready to wake them up. Please talk to them and let them know what has happened. Were they, err, traumatized?"

"Not yet, and now that the bastards are dead, they won't be. Please wake them up."

The first one was woken up. The sight of the aliens freaked her out, but Kenadi managed to calm her down.

"I am Kibill Cranis, age eleven."

"I am Frani Fong, age twelve."

"I am Kisha Wing, age fourteen."

"I am Midiline Fong, age thirteen."

"I am Chana Miduri, age fifteen."

"I am Hanaki Raice, age sixteen. Where are we?"

Kenadi Minga said, "The ship we were on was damaged, and we are the only ones that survived. They are real aliens, and there are some others. One even has giant worms growing out of her head. They all only have two eyes. Kayaice, my little sister, did not survive, but they will be able to make a clone of her."

"What is that?"

"It will look just like her, but it will be reborn as a baby and have no previous memories as Kayaice."

"I liked Kayaice, but she was always sad."

"Some memories are probably best forgotten. They have some other Forandicate people that they rescued from another ship. They were members of the Marku; have you heard of them?"

"I thought they were scary and evil?"

"No, the people who said that were actually the scary and evil people. The aliens, this person is Captain Robinson; they seem like good people. They have set up an area for us, and we can venture out and see the rest of the ship after we get used to the rooms they made for us."

"What will we do? Will they have a school for us?"

"They cheated and taught you the language while you slept."

"Can they do that for algebra while I sleep?"

"I... I don't know, can you?"

Luna said, "Hello, I am Luna; I run the ship. While asleep, you learned the oral language of trade talk and the fundamentals of the written language. You should recognize the alphabet and be able to sound out some simple words. You were also taught about fifty written words that are safety-related. I will schedule you for some online classes to learn more; after that, we can set up a more structured classroom. We don't use sleep learning for everything; you will have to show us what you know, and we will schedule some classes. What have you already learned?"

Hanaki Raice said, "Mostly we were taught sex positions and acts, but we never did any; we were supposed to be pure when…"

I said, "That is not a required act, and if those assholes were not already dead, they would be very quickly. The people who you were… Ah, being prepared for, they were bad people, but now they are gone. Luna, find out if we have any psychologists in the crew and bring them up to speed on this mess. Also, get the captain's niece, Zenner Cheasobod, over here. This probably needs a female close to their age. Let her know what had been done. Give her anything she needs, and let her structure some training classes for these. This gets worse the more we learn."

Zenner showed up in a few minutes, and I left them alone.

"Luna, I am done here. I need to do something-anything else to clear my mind; what is on the agenda?"

"You want to visit with the Special Forces while they are practicing hand-to-hand combat and get the crap beat out of you?"

"Right now, that sounds tempting, but I am sure I will regret it tomorrow. What else?"

"The science crew is assembling a new drone for me. It looks a lot like T-1000 right about now. They haven't started the skin overlay."

"No, I have a hard enough time sleeping after seeing the last almost finished product. The robo-skeletal version sounds nasty. All chrome and with human-looking teeth?"

"No, this version has a white ceramic coating over all the metal structures, so it looks more like steam-punk skeletal."

"What are the major differences between this and the last one?"

"The ship, and therefore, I cannot go with you to the moon. This will be redundantly quantum-linked, so it should be fine to accompany you. It went down in sensations, and it went up in strength. The Ghost Ships forbid me approaching with the main ship… They didn't say I couldn't go with you as an Avatar."

"And you are directly linked to the ship, so if we need anything, you can respond quickly.   Will your Avatar be ready when we get there?"

"Yes, but I am sacrificing cosmetics and sensation response for speed and power.   The old Avatar will be kept as a backup.

Anderson said, "I heard the last part of that conversation; I thought her Avatar was supposed to improve with each new version?"

"It was supposed to be; this was rushed together.   For the height of 5'6", I should weigh 125 for this build; I will top the scales at 255.   The frame is titanium, and some parts are made from tool steel. I make a crappy Terminator, but I should be a little stronger than a human."

"It seems like everyone is tossing every weapon they have at this."

"We are. Oh, I can also speak the Ogre language."

"Great, you can tell us when they say they are politely readying the axe to chop us up with."

"Not a desired dialog, but well within the predicted normals. Captain, your presence is requested in room 7-21.   Wear your hard suit.   This is set up temporally as a vacuum firing range.   They want to demonstrate some weapons."

'Oh joy, I get to see weapons fired."

"You will be commanding people who will be fighting Ogres, so you need to know what the weapons do and look like when fired."

Sigh, "You are probably correct; I will stop at my room and then head there."

I trudged back to my room and got dressed in my hard suit.

One would think that someone stomping through hallways wearing a full vacuum hard suit would attract attention, but on a ship populated with a dozen different alien races, no one paid any attention to me.

Eventually, I arrived at the designated room (Luna sent me turn-by-turn directions).

"This must be the place." There were three other people in hard suits waiting outside the recently added airlock door.

I recognized Tomoe Ishida's voice when she spoke, "We are taking shifts seeing how this works. We get one test shot, and then we save the live ones for action. Lilly Suzuki already got her shot. Keijko Okada is in there now. I am up next; should be only a few…"

THUD!

"Looks like we are up. You and Anderson get to watch me as Frigiila, one of the trainers, walks me through my one test shot. Takes them a few minutes to patch the target up between each shot."

A few minutes later, the airlock door opened, and three people exited; then we entered.

The room was dimly lit, and at the end of a long hallway was an eighteen-foot tall Ogre made out of some type of thin metal, and over it was a printed image. It was the image of the little girl Ogre, only the size was blown up to be eighteen feet tall.

The center of mass of the Ogre was patched up, with several layers of replacement sheet metal and paper with printed images over it. The target looked like the chest cavity had taken multiple hits, and one side of the face was missing, but they must not have had a replacement panel for that.

The first thing that happened was that some Sulimon pointed at a pressure sensor on the wall. We were at very close to zero, and the gauge was dropping. Then, I was directed to stand in the spectator area, over to the side.

Tomoe Ishida was walking through dry-firing the weapon, and it looked like a giant hollow tube you fired on your shoulder. The instructor showed her a kneeling position and then made sure everyone was clear of the exhaust from the back of the weapon.

The target was on some type of motorized cable system. At one point, it was pulled rapidly towards Tomoe Ishida. It stopped short five feet away and then slowly retreated to the back wall. A huge, angled, thick metal deflector covered that.

The instructor walked Tomoe Ishida through it about three times, and then, the last time, everyone stood clear of her. It went the same as the practice runs. The target was charging her position, and then **BAM!** It was all over.

By all over, most of us were knocked down or almost over. The instructor didn't even seem to wobble. Anderson somehow stayed standing. Tomoe Ishida slid forward and needed to use an arm to catch herself.

Then I noticed the target. It was now missing a large hole; it was large enough to put your hand through, and the hole was over the center of the chest.

The post-firing clean-up took a few minutes, and then we exited, seeing three new people in hard suits ready to take our place. One of them was Princess Domonis.

She started unlatching her helmet as soon as she was out past the airlock double doors. I removed my helmet as well.

"Well, that was my first time firing anything in a vacuum. The exhaust blow-back was exaggerated, but being near a wall or rock will have the same effect. What did you think?"

"We're screwed; the one time I had a real Ogre charge us, it was over in the blink of an eye. I think we got a few dozen rounds off, and one of us was dead, the other missing an arm. I was lucky; I was only missing a few fingers. I think we need to fire from no warning, and the kneeling position may be stable, but what if they attacked from the other side?"

She just stared at me. "Oh crap, I forgot that you have fought one before. This was so we know how to operate in a vacuum and stabilize the weapon."

"And the computer fired a FIM-92 Stinger pre-aimed directly down the door the beast charged out of. It took four body bags to fit all the parts, and some had to be scraped off the walls and ceilings. You need speed first, accuracy second, and collateral damage is something you worry about after the body parts have landed. If I am standing directly behind you, shoot the weapon. If I am beside you, and it comes from the side, shoot it. Don't worry about me or the exhaust."

"It ejects a large hot plug out the back after firing."

"And guns eject hot brass out the side when firing. If your brass is hitting your buddy, you ignore it; he will move if he needs to. The hard suit will either protect everyone or it won't. The Ogre doesn't care. The oversized battle axe does a hell of a lot worse than anything you can imagine. This weapon shoots a section of pipe. You are basically taking a core sample from an Ogre. If the Ogre is female and wearing a tungsten bra, aiming where you did may just jiggle her boobs. What do you aim at next?"

"Huh?"

"The first team is now a marmalade carpet stain. What do you shoot at for your shot?"

"Arr, Face shot, the helmet is probably breakable. What would you shoot at, sir?"

I smiled; this was the first time I think she actually respected me as her captain. "Every spacesuit I have ever seen has weak areas, the side under the ribs, the neck, something that has to be flexible; chances are hitting it hard will vent something. If it is standing next to some machinery, make a split-second judgment: Is it something that will explode if you shoot it? If you think it's male, aim lower than you normally would."

She smiled, "I know many ways to kill a man, and I have used that one before."

"You probably did a lot of stealth and planning. The monster Axe they wield will slice the turret off of an M-1 Abrams tank. The battle lasted just over one second. One Army Ranger fired a Barrett M107A1 50BMG in full auto mode at it. Doctor Smith put half a clip from her M-16 into it. I stood by with a useless stunner. The Ogre, a frocking little girl, the equivalent of a twelve-year-old, went directly for the largest threat and neutralized him in less than a second. I think our best weapon is Princess Domonis."

"Why?"

"If she sees an Ogre come at her, her first action would be to rip off the latches on the Ogre's helmet; what happens then?"

"The Ogre is dead."

"One Ogre is dead; he just may not realize it, and it may still manage to kill a few more of us before it realizes it's dead. There may be a few dozen behind it. They may fight one-on-one, more likely, they will fight in a coordinated group."

Anderson said, "The captain is right; the battle was over for a well-armed and trained Army Ranger in less than a second. If you can, shove an M72 LAR up its ass and pull the trigger. If you may survive, that would be a story to tell the grandkids."

I said, "Luna, are there any weapons you can produce with your printers?"

"I will look into it. What is the weight limit I should impose?"

She smiled, "Figure double what the Captain can carry."

Luna said, "I will limit it to what you can carry when running and fully loaded wearing a hard spacesuit. Our Captain has highly modified DNA, and while he may not look like it, his strength is a lot more than you would expect."

I said, "It is?"

"You have been hitting the gym every other day for an hour, and you have been letting me set the resistance forces. Yes, you are improving. Anderson still exceeds you, but he exercises almost two hours daily."

I looked at my biceps, "They don't seem any larger?"

"The average amount you are lifting is 40% more than before you became a snake hair fang pincushion and science experiment. This has been less than three months."

"I need a weapon that I can constantly carry, and it needs to make an Ogre stop and take notice with one shot.   What do you have?"

"Nothing that meets those requirements…   I have found something online.   I am pinging the military and seeing if anyone has it."

.. .. ..

A few minutes later, "I contacted Earth to see what they had. They will provide us with twelve Smith and Wesson model 500 revolvers that use the .500 Magnum cartridges.   I ordered enough cartridge cases to keep all the military people happy.   They will be directing a freighter from Earth just to deliver them.   We meet with the cargo freighter just before entering the forbidden zone.   They are based on the Russian powder and primers that work in a vacuum. Supposedly, it is harsh on handguns but harsher on what you aim it at.   You will be sore as hell, but it shouldn't shatter your wrist."

Tomoe Ishida said, "If you are lucky.   I have fired the regular loads, not the vacuum crap.   I still had a hairline fracture after only five rounds."

"I will take that. It sounds like something that should at least sting an Ogre.   The A-10 Gatling gun will, however, stop one."

"They are sending us four more. Two will be for modified HMMWVs converted to electric, and two A-10 Gatling guns will be welded to the new ship's outer hull. The expectation is that they will survive a few short bursts. They did a test, and the door to the shuttle the first Ogre was on was breached in 0.115 seconds in one burst.   We don't know how armored the ones we meet will be.

.. .. ..

The trip to the rendezvous location went without incident.   We met the freighter, and we unloaded the guns.   We also offloaded all of the Forandicate except for two.   Laido Severit and Lena Motoko both wanted to stay on our ship for a while longer.   We unloaded the artificial womb that contained Kayaice Loungerone, the unborn sister of Friddot Lounger.

79

I said, "You realize we are heading into a battle?"

"We are both soldiers. We are also refugees of a destroyed race. We want to go with you to show you our appreciation for rescuing us."

"Your race is probably not destroyed; there should be survivors. The Federation will send a set of search and recovery ships to survey what remains. I will allow you to remain on this ship. The ship doing the search and destroy mission will all be combatants. What we will be fighting if we meet them is far beyond what anyone alone can handle. That is why we will take every opportunity to combine our abilities."

"Then maybe we can help?"

"How? We have seen nothing your race can do that the others can't do."

Lena Motoko pointed at her eyes, all three of them. You have scanned us in your medical pods. Has your computer failed to figure out what our eyes do?"

Luna said, "I assumed it was vision-related."

"It is; however, each of our eyes sees a different spectrum of light. One is the spectrum you call visible light. The second is in the infrared, and the other is in the microwave spectrum."

"You see in microwaves?"

"Ah, you may spot something we can't."

Luna said, "I can monitor the full spectrum of those bands."

"Yes, but you haven't spent your entire life seeing using those bands. You detect signals and look for data; they will see things you cannot."

Luna said, "I am slightly offended, but yes, it may help. I believe your goal is to take anything that improves the odds of success. That is why you have an almost random collection of weapons."

"Our one experience with Ogres was one nerdy little girl.   Not all of us survived that.   When is the special ship from the Ghost Ships arriving?"

"It is waiting for us at the edge of the Forbidden Zone. As soon as we undock from the freighter, we will head there.   We should arrive within the hour."

"I feel like we are forgetting something important, something we should bring that may help our odds."

"I will summon Jennifer Woods and Doctor Cora Smith to the conference room.   Anyone else I should summon?"

"All the usual bridge crew…   Include Arshiya and Sophia Nikolaou.   Maybe one of them can think of something we missed."

THE FORBIDDEN ZONE

Luna said, "The freighter has left, and we are heading to the rendezvous location to meet up with the new ship. We have the two HMMWVs modified to include the A-10 Gatling guns in the Shuttle bay. Everyone you requested is here in the conference room. What is the plan?"

"The plan is to destroy the damn FTL capable derelict. We are forbidden from entering the star system with an FTL capable drive or even with an AI that includes any knowledge of how to build an FTL system. We are also forbidden from simply doing an aerial bombardment. Kelapaton and Princess Domonis are the primary means of destroying the ship. We need backups and alternatives. We also need to potentially rescue anyone that had the misfortune to crash their ship on that moon."

Luna said, "The Ghost Ships refer to the Ogres as their Creators. We don't know, but we suspect they have some residual core programming that prevents them from just wiping out their Creators. Or maybe they have some ethical beliefs that killing your Creator is a line they should not cross."

"Anderson, what is the status of the weapons?"

We have received the new pistols. We added reinforcing to the one shooting range and will cycle everyone through to fire three sets of five rounds. We will do this in normal air, not in the vacuum chamber. The odds of developing a leak are too high. We will figure out something before we meet up with the special ship. The medical pods and the two A-10 Gatling guns for the hull exterior are ready to install. The HMMWVs will be attached under the ship's body, and we will drop them the last three feet. The tires are filled with steel slinkies so that the ride will be rougher than normal. The moon has some air, but not enough to support us without suits. We have fired half the oversized ventilators, the pipe shooters in training. The Marines have twelve M72 LARs modified to work in the partial vacuum on the moon. One of the Marines has also brought an oversized wrist-rocket slingshot."

"Let me guess, his first name is David?"

"Wow, you must be psychic. It will, however, be the quietest range weapon we have."

Luna said, "I have an Avatar I will use, but this one looks like shit. The biological outer layer will not be ready in time, so I have an outer layer of silicon. It looks like the unholy child of a T-1000 Terminator and a low-end sex doll."

Jennifer Woods said, "I have already sent a video of it to Earth, and the convention crowd actually loves it."

Doctor Cora Smith said, "She will be wearing a spacesuit over the monstrosity, so it doesn't look too bad. All the suits and the HMMWVs have been painted a camouflaged set of grey colors. Your names are in flat black on the front and back so we can identify everyone. Everyone will have clear faceplates. The only lights will be hand-held. There will be none mounted on helmets. There is supposed to be enough air to carry sound. We will only use quantum radios and no RF bands. They have only two bands. The first is fed to multiplexers, and it transmits to everyone. The second is only to Keith and Jake. They have one extra band to Princess Domonis."

Anderson said. "We will start in mode-1, stealth. Don't shoot unless ordered to. At some point, I expect we will go to mode-2, where we shoot any Ogres we see as soon as we see them. There is a mode-3, and that is to destroy the ship at any cost. The last mode is retreat. We leave the HMMWVs behind. They can be operated remotely, and they include a destruct charge."

I said, "What about recovering anyone from the ship if survivors are in stasis pods?"

"If possible, do that during the first two modes. Mode-3 means the shit has hit the fan. The Marines have a motto, 'No Man Left Behind.' We don't have that luxury on this mission. We will not stop to recover any bodies. We may even leave someone alive behind when we leave. Everyone will be carrying three of the Sulimon hand grenades with them. These are smaller than the

Earth ones and have a much higher yield. If you are left behind and alive, save the last one for yourself."

That put a somber mood on everyone in the room.

"The Sulimon grenades start a four-second timer when you pull the pin; there is no pop-up handle. They are more thermal and less shrapnel. If something can possibly burn, they will set it on fire."

Anderson said, "Captain, you get to try the wrist cracker as soon as this meeting is over. Hearing protection will be provided."

"Oh, joy..."

.. .. ..

I test-fired the Smith and Wesson model 500, and it didn't break my wrist. I was still really sore.

Anderson said, "That was a lot worse than I remember from the time I fired one of those years ago."

Doctor Cora Smith said, "Yeah, they made special bullets for these. Teflon coated, steel jacketed over a spent Uranium core. So try not to shoot anyone on our side."

Luna announced, "Exiting FTL in three minutes, prepare for entry to the Forbidden Zone."

"Where are we meeting up."

Luna said, "First stop is any medical pod for a 'quick purge' and then to docking port-A. The drones will take care of operating the HMMWV Winches and release hardware. They will be unmanned when we drop them. Then report to your quarters and get suited up in the new hard Suits. Unfortunately, you are all required to fully connect the urine collection hardware. We don't know how long this will take, but the non-FTL part of the ride to the moon is almost three hours."

"Does the shuttle have a restroom?"

"Yes, but it is a zero-G waste facility. I assume you would rather avoid it."

.. .. ..

After the medical pod purge and suiting up, we were all milling around. Finally, we exited FTL.

The Forbidden Zone didn't look any different from any other part of space.

At the rendezvous location was what looked like a derelict mid-sized spacecraft. It was unusually dark, almost jet-black in color. It looked like two spacecraft that were docked…

Anderson burst out laughing.

"Yeah, I see it; it is the most phallic-shaped thing I have ever seen, A giant black…"

Lilly Suzuki said, "Don't say it!"

Luna said, "Ignoring the obvious, it is a large cigar-shaped spacecraft, and the landing legs are folded up under it. The FTL drive is attached at the back and has two partially circular hemispheres. The coloring and shape are to increase the stealth effect. The FTL drive will deliver to the planet, immediately release the cigar-shaped object, and depart. It will only return if you make it back to the same area in space, where it will re-dock and leave as soon as it can. Hopefully, you will not be pursued. I am docking with the craft now, and the drones will begin attaching the two HMMWVs and the drop sky cranes. As soon as it is docked, we will start loading it. Primary loading will be the medical pods and universal power hookups in case we need to take the one from the derelict. While it may look like a derelict, it is supposedly structurally sound. The Ghost Ships were good enough to add mounting pads and power/data connections for where we are adding the two A-10 Gatling guns and the drop lifts. We should be ready to depart in ninety-five minutes. Travel time in FTL is only ninety-two minutes. Travel time to the moon is an additional eighty-five minutes."

There was a loud thunk as the overly phallic ship docked.

"The drones are away. Cycling the hatch."

The inner airlock door opened, followed one minute later by the outer airlock door. What was inside was the open airlock doors to a dimly lit ship.

Luna said, "We will add more lights; the ship is sparsely equipped. Drones will move the medical pods into place and add extra lighting. Sleeping racks, and just that. Three high and, from the look of it, cramped for some of us."

Anderson said, "Six foot two, I wonder who that will be? What do we do?"

"The trauma kits and the weapons to start. We will be epoxying the hardware cases in place, so there will be no welding and, hopefully, no drilling. With luck, we will abandon this monster... Thing in a day or two."

Lilly Suzuki said, "What is the layout?"

"An oversized cargo airlock on one end, the large single hatch on the front that folds down into a ramp. The back is all the medical pods, and room for two more in case we extract any from the derelict on the moon. It has actually had two restrooms. The zero-G one is on the right, and the unusable standard gravity one is on the left. The old bucket does not have replicators or even recyclers. It is topped off with 230 gallons of distilled water and a waste tank that can hold 290 gallons. As soon as the weapons are on, load the bulk supplies, food, and toiletries. Everyone will have four days of underwear, and if you need to be in here past ten days, the CO_2 scrubbers will start to fail."

I said, "All of this seems obsolete?"

"It is, intentionally; the Ghost Ships don't put it at 50% odds of us returning. I put it higher."

Someone yelled from the inside, "We will need toilet paper; this really is obsolete."

"The boxes are labeled. The ones for the restrooms indicate which type. Assume you will be stuck in here for a week; hope for a day."

.. .. ..

Eventually, it was loaded, the two electric HMMWVs were mounted on the outside, and the tensioners had everything clamped down and secured. "The Gatling gun on the front had an X-Y pivot on it, and it could swing 57.5 degrees left of right and left, as well as 12.5 degrees of up and down."

The food packs were all secured by netting, and every day had the same high shelf life food as the next. The only difference was that the last-day meals were supposed to be better. Best case, that was the only meal we ate; worst case, it was the 'last' meal."

One final check, and then the thuds of the airlock hatches being sealed. Then, the artificial gravity from the main ship was shut off with a clunk, and we started drifting away.

We were lucky; no one needed to quickly remove their helmets and clear any vomit… Yet.

About two minutes later, the FTL kicked in, and this was the old-style FTL. I counted three helmets being rapidly removed, and everyone had the cleaning kits next to them.

"I don't know why we didn't all remove the helmets before entering FTL. Then we could just use a barf-bag."

Luna's Avatar said, "For the same reason, we will all have the suits on when they are done clearing them. This hull may be structurally sound, but something unexpected could fail at any time. That said, conserve water if you are cleaning up in the restrooms."

The ninety-two minutes in FTL went by uneventfully. When we exited FTL, the FTL engine disconnected almost immediately, and we were drifting alone within thirty seconds.

Luna said, "Engaging the sub-light engines, please secure yourselves. I don't know how rough these will be. Travel time to the moon will be 88 minutes. 5, 4, 3, 2, 1, now!"

Actually, it wasn't all that bad.

"You will have forty-four minutes of 0.85G accelerating towards the moon, a sixty-second flip, and then forty-three minutes of deceleration. The last four minutes before we hit the atmosphere is when we have the final commit or abort, and we hopefully identify where the target and where any hostiles are."

I said, "Anderson, you will be running the tactical display. Get us some status as soon as the planet is in scanner range. Those are probably obsolete junk as well. I will be in the seat beside you, and Lilly Suzuki and Princess Domonis will be behind us. I doubt anyone else will be able to read your handheld display."

Princess Domonis said, "Why are we doing this? I am doing this because Mother said to. Why are the Ghost ships not just bombing the crap out of them?"

Luna said, "The Ghost Ships are normally pacifists. Someone was probably on the ship when it went down, so per their code, they don't like to kill an innocent bystander intentionally. However, waiting until the stasis pods are guaranteed to fail would mean they can lob a few asteroids with impunity. We need to remove the survivors, if any exist, or at least confirm there are none. It is better if we eliminate the FTL drive entirely on our own, at least from their AI viewpoint."

"And sending us in to possibly die is okay?"

"We don't understand exactly how they think. We, meaning the Earth, get some reward when this is over. No one has told me what that is. Anderson, Princess Domonis, do either of you know?"

"No."

"Nope, but I suspect Mother is getting something out of it as well, and not just the Earth."

Anderson said, "Sensors are online, I show three hot spots, I don't see the derelict."

I said, "So if we can't detect it, then hopefully the Ogres can't detect it. If they already found it, I assume we would be told to turn back?"

"Yes, they are monitoring the movements. I have a tactical map showing where they have been. It looks like the Ogres have gone

88

after the intentionally crashed distraction ship. That was crashed 200 years ago. It contains crew that were deceased long before the crash and a fake version of FTL that would never work. It also impacted at a high velocity, leaving a very easy-to-find impact crater. The real derelict did a soft landing on the side that faces away from the planet. They only put up their first satellites within the last 100 years."

"Great, they have had space travel for longer than the Earth. Most of our high-tech equipment is from alien sources."

"Do we know what they have for governments? For stability? Are there warring factions?"

"They haven't provided us with a lot of information. Possibly, they haven't kept track of what the Ogres are doing. Or they may are hiding something."

"You think there is a chance the Ogres are not violent?"

"Possible, but not likely. Wait, even Pirates could be reasoned with in some cases. The first set of the Pirate's Code was supposedly written by some Portuguese buccaneer Bartolomeu Português. The first recorded set belonged to George Cusack. And no, the Pirates of the Caribbean movies made up most of what they said. The real rules covered things like discipline and division of stolen goods. The Ogres must have some order if they are systematically expanding their technology level. They must have scientists and technicians. Not just people that chop you into little itty bits."

"So, depending on who we meet, they may be able to reason with them?"

"We failed miserably with a little Ogre girl. If we see one with skulls hanging from their belt, I say shoot first."

"Luna, what is our trajectory? Will they be able to detect us?"

"They may be able to detect us when we are thirty minutes away, but they won't be able to tell where on the moon we are headed until five minutes before we land. Given their reported drive technology, we will have at least sixty-eight minutes before they can arrive. If they have defensive weapons, and they did something like fired surface-to-surface missiles on the moon, we have a lot less time, and if we manage to survive a missile attack, we bug out immediately."

"Yeah, I guess we really are the invaders, and we are out to destroy what they consider valuable resources. Let me know as soon as you think they have detected us. Are you monitoring any of their communications?"

"The noise from the planet is so massive I can't tell much apart. I see several communication channels from the moon and someplace on the planet. I can't even hack into the damn data channels with this limited crap hardware they provided."

"How is your Avatar doing? Is it holding up well?"

"I screwed up. I look like a sex doll from the recycling pile. The suit thermal regulators were sized for a human body that produces the same heat output as a 100W bulb and, under exertion, close to 500W of power. I am producing 1,200W, or about as much as a hair dryer. The silicon is splitting, and the foam under it is ripping." I will remain operational, but I will look like a cheap horror movie prop after one too many Halloweens."

Then Luna announced, "All hands, prepare for the gravity flip and the start of deceleration."

Then we were in zero-G and then rotating.

Anderson said, "Prepare for the start of deceleration."

The flip was completed, and gravity returned.

"Repositioning the sensors… We have sensors, but still, no indication that they have detected us… yet."

I said, "Can you detect the derelict?"

"Not yet, but we know exactly where it landed. I think the Ghost Ships impacted a meteor into the moon a few centuries ago. Everything is under a uniform layer of dust."

Luna said, "That sounds like something they would have done. The data I have just received shows it as a Meduala scout, class BB-7, a little smaller than my original Pathfinder-171. The ship is 275 feet long, which would have had a max of three stasis pods, the old 'B' generation. Unfortunately, they sometimes crammed in a crew of six, but only three had stasis. I ran the location by the Meduala before we left, and they don't have any record of it. That old, it could just be poor bookkeeping, or it may have had a sketchy cargo. If anyone was in the stasis pods, they are at the extreme limits of survivability."

.. .. ..

"We are about to stop deceleration. Then, we will light up the moon's thin atmosphere with our plasma trail. Still no traffic on the radio channels… We are back at zero gravity. The next gravity you feel will be the push-back of what passes for the atmosphere."

A minute later, that started, and it was initially barely noticeable. Then, it slowly started increasing and pressing us down against the floor. Outside the few portholes, it was now flickering white-hot plasma.

"They have noticed us, and their radio chatter is now all over the place. Oh goody, they are sending out two separate crews to respond."

Anderson said, "I have detected the derelict. It looks like it did a hard landing but is intact."

"Take us down close to the enough that we can drop the HMMWVs, then land this ship as close as possible to the derelict. The situation evaluation and FTL destruction are the main tasks. Princess Domonis, then you are up, and you get to make the ship into something that Kelapaton can handle. We are now approaching the derelict. The plasma effects have stopped. Both HMMWVs show as online. We are starting the sky-crane deployment. Both are deploying correctly. Wait, we have a hang-up on one of the cables. Contingency plan B: We detached that cable. The HMMWVs are on their way down, but they are bouncing around. One has hit the other HMMWV. Almost on the ground, we are releasing the clamps. We are separated. We are now releasing the winches. All are clear, and we are now preparing for landing. The HMMWV's statuses are somehow still all in the green. We are on the Ogre's moon."

THE OGRE'S MOON

Luna said, "The door is opening. Pressure shows as 5.5PSI, Thirty-Three percent Carbon Dioxide, and only two percent oxygen. The temperature is a balmy 50F (10C). It has abundant small scrub plants; probably safest to pretend they are carnivorous or poisonous and leave them alone."

Anderson said, "A nice, beautiful, crisp fall day, except for the poisonous atmosphere and the alien Ogres heading our way. Recon team, get to high ground and see what you can find with those triple eyes of yours. Get those HMMWVs over here. Shit, barely out of the parking lot, and you dinged up the fenders. The derelict is 200 yards ahead. Watch for sharp debris and metal, anything that can slice a suit open. Extraction team, find the door and the escape hatch and see if the manual releases work. Bring the power cutter in case it doesn't. The HMMWV has the Gatling gun if we need to turn the hatch into Swiss cheese."

Princess Domonis said, "If you can't open the door, I can do that much quicker than the cutters."

"Go. Go. Go."

Everyone went running, leaving Patti and me alone.

"Err, what is my job?"

Pattie said, "Mine is alien communications. We have a while before they get here. You are the technical lead. You are good at spotting things that are out of place or missing. Let's get over to the derelict and watch the real fun. We should be there in two minutes."

.. .. ..

It took closer to three minutes, and the landscape was very rocky. There was some scattered debris on one side. Some tanks had burst on landing. As we arrived, two Marines in suits called, "The manual door controls are inoperative; you are up, Domonis."

They ran for cover, and I watched in awe as what was a door and part of the frame liquified and reshaped itself into a ramp leading into the dark interior.

"Watch for sharp edges. Extraction crew, get in and attach the magnetic lights as you go."

I keyed the broadcast channel, "Check for live power when you go in there; rails may be exposed and still hot. The layout probably doesn't exactly match the specifications. Look for recent repairs or modifications."

It took only two minutes, but the report came back. There were three stasis pods, and only one was still viable. That showed alarms for just about everything. Power, consumables, battery failure, and unresolved medical issues. The drones disconnected it and hooked it up to a portable power unit.

"We found the FTL drive, and it is almost intact. The computer in this is ancient, and it was based on crystalline memory. Mister Sledgehammer has erased the core. Princess Domonis, we have actual hardcopy manuals. Can your abilities make these go away? There isn't enough oxygen in the air to start any type of fire. It looks like paper, but this may be some type of plastic sheeting."

"Whatever it was, I can mix in some chunks of metal and effectively grind and blend it all together. I can't directly cause heating with my abilities. I can only bend and distort metals, but they get hot quickly when I do that."

"Do it. The stasis pod is on its way out, and they will winch/drag it to the fold-down carrier on the back of the HMMWV."

Luna said, "Update: the first of the two incoming groups is now about seventeen minutes away; the second will be less than ten minutes behind them."

"The pod has more alarms going off now!"

"Ignore them; get it into the landing ship now. Worry about the alarms later. Domonis, as soon as you are done cutting out paper dolls and playing paper shredder, get the FTL drive turned into an oversized paperweight. What is that?"

"We are not sure; it's not Meduala tech, and it looks like they were transporting it. It looks like a miniature stasis pod, and it's much higher technology level than anything on this ship should have."

"Put it in the ship with the failing stasis pod. Captain, it's your call. Do we shoot first, or try and talk to them and then shoot?"

I said, "Luna, can we talk to them on their radio channels? What are they saying?"

"We can transmit, and they should be able to receive us. The chatter is about things like a chance for Glory. Something about how to divide up the souvenirs, or maybe it is salvage. One was wondering what we would look like."

Lilly Suzuki said, "Wait until they are two minutes away, and then say, 'The aliens wonder if they are worthy.' If we are lucky, that will make them approach slower and spend more time trying to figure out what we are."

I said, "Or it may make them speed up to see who gets the first aliens to rape, pillage and then rip apart."

One of the marines said, "Crap, the stasis pod is smoking. We are thirty seconds away from the ship."

I yelled, "Do not enter the ship with a pod that may explode. Stop twenty feet away and do a hard forced eject. Rip the cover off of it if you have to. Then, stick a respirator over the patient and run them to the first medical pod. Do not close the ship doors and pressurize. We don't have time to recycle the air. A little carbon dioxide exposure should be something the medical pod can handle."

Anderson said, "All the scouts are now returning, prep for evacuation."

Princess Domonis said, "The FTL is now a compressed ball of slag. Where do you want Kelapaton to send it?"

"Aim it at that jagged outcropping over there. With luck, the cliff face will collapse after it impacts."

Kelapaton said, "I will need assistance after I do this. I will be non-responsive."

"You two go over there and grab her."

As soon as they reached her, the large ball of metal turned into an ion trail, and the cliff face exploded like it was hit with a nuclear bomb.

Luna said, "We have their attention. I recommend against taunting them with promises of willing alien females unless First Lieutenant Suzuki is planning on staying behind."

"Fuck you!"

"Shut up, everyone, head to the ship as fast as possible. Luna, what is their ETA?"

"Jones and Powell and carrying Domonis/Kelapaton to the remaining HMMWV. The other is positioned on high ground to give cover fire when needed. We should leave ninety seconds before they arrive."

That was the plan, but it didn't go as planned.

"The second HMMWV is now in a hard fault state. We are abandoning it. We need help carrying the unresponsive Domonis/Kelapaton."

Luna ran to help them. The rest of us ran as fast as possible while wearing full armored spacesuits. That was a slow jog speed, and we were all breathing hard as we approached our ship. The unknown artifact was stowed, and the Marines were in positions around the ship with what looked like the LARs.

Luna said, "They will arrive before we are ready to lift off. The reconnaissance people have all entered the ship. It is ready for immediate departure. They are securing the loads. The patient is a female meduala, and she has been transferred to the medical pod. It can't give a status on her yet. There are too many priority things to do after she breathed concentrated carbon dioxide. She is boxed and loaded. That's all we can do. Captain, get your ass moving. You are needed on the ship, not holding back with us."

I wasn't intentionally staying with them. I was out of breath. The thought of approaching Ogres was a tremendous incentive, and I ran like my life depended on it. It probably did.

As I entered the ship, I saw that Anderson and the other Marines were running just behind me and that a single individual in a spacesuit was carrying Princess Domonis. It took a second to realize it was Luna's Avatar, and then, off in the distance, I saw the Ogres ship approaching.

It was a combination of two things. Underneath was a massive tank-like armored crawler, and on top of it was the portion with the rocket engines on it. It resembled the transporter from the old Science Fiction TV show Space 1999. Only updated to be a tactical military way of delivering heavy armor. I made a quick decision.

"Wait until it is on or near the ground and deploy the ground transporter. Then, fire everything we have at the rocket carrier. With luck, you hit the fuel tank or an engine. Luna, send them the following message, 'We have been trying to reach you about your car's extended warranty.'"

Anderson said, "Are you intentionally provoking them to shoot first?"

Luna said, "They have started charging weapons."

.. .. ..

The ship was about 1,500 feet away and almost at the ground when a turret on it opened fire at the first of the HMMWVs. Fortunately, it was the nonoperational one. It disintegrated in an explosion of debris.

We returned fire from the Gatling guns on the ship and the surviving HMMWV, and the two Marines to either side of the ship both fired a LAR at almost the same time.

The carrier veered off to one side, and cables still attached to the ground transporter flipped that over onto its side, the cables severed, and the carrier flew off sideways to maybe 100 feet before colliding with the ground and rolling away in a cloud of dust.

Then the ground transporter opened a hatch, and three Ogres in massive spacesuits climbed out. When they were out, the last one handed the others massive battle axes. Then they pulled the last one out by his battle axe.

The Gatling guns shifted over to targeting the almost twenty-foot-tall monsters in space suites. Our side was now deploying some smaller weapons; these were probably the Ninjas with the Sulimon pipe shooters.

The first two shots were misses, the third shot was a hit, and it was on the arm of one of the Ogres.

Whatever the suits were made of was tough. The impact drew blood, but something designed to rip through a shuttle did a minor flesh wound. They were shifting over to more of the LARs. The Gatling guns should tear apart a heavy tank, and they were having the same effect a 22 short pistol did when facing a bear. One lucky shot shattered the Ogre helmet face plate, and they were as ugly as my nightmares remembered them. Then the Gatling gun ripped the face to shreds. The Ogre went down, probably dead, but we had two uninjured Ogres remaining.

Then, a shot from a LAR hit one on the wrist. The explosion took the hand clean off, and…. "Where is the third one? I think he is behind cover."

Luna said, "Prepare for immediate departure; the second ship is coming in hot."

Everything became a blur after that. We started shutting the hatches and lifting off as soon as everyone was on board. I saw the second ship rapidly approaching, and then it was eclipsed by the Unharmed Ogre and its oversized battle axe. There was a massive clang; the entire ship was slammed downward, and then it somehow, thankfully, lifted off and shot off up into the sky.

The second HMMWV on the ground was now shattered, and the one remaining Gatling gun shifted from the lone Ogre to the rapidly approaching ship.

Then, it was two parts; they jettisoned the crawler, which fell several hundred yards and then crashed hard on the ground. The transporter started moving in a direct line towards our ship.

Loud banging sounds and jarring thuds now shook our ship. I saw light shining through holes where there shouldn't be holes. The whine of the Gatling gun then cut off and was replaced by a bone-jarring thud.

"We have lost the rear Gatling gun. It did some damage to the transporter, and it is now veering off, and it looks like it will make an emergency landing."

Anderson yelled, "Everyone call out, is anyone else injured?"

"Domonis/Kelapaton is still non-responsive, but I don't see any wounds."

Lilly Suzuki said, "Second Lieutenant Tomoe Ishida is dead; one of their rounds had split her head open."

"We have another body, crap, it's the fricking Terminator."

Luna's crumpled body spoke, "Sorry, that is me. This body is no longer functional, but the head will still work for a while. The battery is failing but should last until we are docked with the FTL drive. We have cleared the thin atmosphere, and we are accelerating away. We are not holding air. Please send out repair crews and patch the holes. The trajectory is locked in. The sub-light drive is running hot. I have changed the trajectory to reduce the current. The course is tied to the drive temperature. ETA to reach the transfer point is now eleven hours. I am entering low power mode to conserve battery; I will wake up in two hours."

Everyone else responded and gave their status. One marine had taken a piece of shrapnel to the stomach, and the suit was patched, but he needed to be in a medical pod to repair the wound. He needed to be out of the suit to enter the chamber.

Anderson said, "Crews are patching the holes. We have found eight large holes. Entrance holes are three inches around, and the exit holes are closer to five."

I was at the data panel, " This bucket only had dual rails. The secondary rail is shorted. The backup power core is..... Oh shit! I am ejecting the secondary core."

Thud!

"It's safely ejected. The primary core is still fully operational."

"How bad was it?"

"We all need to get in the medical pods. We just took the equivalent of a few hundred chest X-rays. I show we lost oxygen tanks four, five, and seven. We also lost all the nitrogen tanks.   I am closing off water tank B, now pumping what remains in it back to tank A. Crap, I am showing a methane leak. Someone see if it is the tank or the piping. Section C, near frame number seventeen or eighteen."

We patched what we could for the next hour and closed off what was leaking.

I had dozed off and awoke to hear a grinder-cutter removing some flaring around one of the holes so the patch would fit.

"How are we doing for suit air?"

"Those are good for another five hours. We will have one section holding air after these last two patches. We can't fix one of the holes in the hull, as it ripped up too much. Kramer is the wounded Marine, and we moved some of the medical pods to the room that should be able to hold pressure."

I stood up to find I was almost floating and only weighed a fraction of what I should.

"What is our acceleration?"

"We usually try for one-G. We are at less than one-third of that. That is stable, so our trip is going to take a lot longer than we planned."

"Is there any chance the Ogres can pursue us?"

"Yes, they could, no they are not... Yet."

"What about Tomoe Ishida?"

"Still very dead. Even immediately putting her in a medical pod wouldn't have changed anything."

"Kramer?"

"So far, he is okay, but his wound is still bleeding."

"Sorry that I fell asleep."

"We are glad it was only sleep.   The back of your helmet is actually dented in.   How is your head?"

"That explains the splitting headache.   I think I am okay.   How is Luna?"

"She now wakes up on the hour and updates us.   We are making up a power connector and will shift her to wall power soon. Her battery is depleted and crapping out."

"What the hell?   I see stars at the end of the hallway."

We opened the door.   No air inside or outside makes it easier to patch some of the holes.   We have a problem, and you may be able to help."

"What?"

"One shot ripped off the FTL docking port on the port side."

I went to the data terminal and brought up the inventory display.

"I don't see any vacuum welding equipment or impulse fabricators."

"No, the Ghost Ships were insistent on what technology level we could bring.   The HMMWV is considered low-tech, and the A-10 Gatling gun is also considered low-tech.   The only high technology item we came with was the FTL drive, which ran off and is now hiding."

"What about the miniature stasis pod artifact, and how is the patient from the normal stasis pod."

"We are not sure; there are a lot of red flags on her condition. I don't think anyone ever ran out of stasis chemicals and drained the power that low and actually lived. The artifact is unexpected. I wonder if the Ghost Ships knew about this. It appears to be a medical/stasis chamber but of unknown alien origin. The power is incredible, and it seems to have one healthy occupant. It will take Luna a while to interface with that and figure out what species it contains. What we do know is that it's tiny. The alien chamber is only thirty-four inches long. It would be a tight fit for a two-year-old. It has locked us out of anything except for what looks like the most basic information screen."

"How did the foodstuffs and other supplies do?"

"We have water but no recycling system. We have oxygen but no carbon dioxide scrubbers except for the manual filters. We are rationing supplies and figure we need to put everyone not needed into medical pods within three days, and then we have supplies for a two-man crew to stay awake for three weeks."

I said, "Yeah, I can see the need for a two-man crew. If something goes wrong, that gives us a backup. I assume they will wear spacesuits most of the time?"

"The restrooms both are intact, but we will be stuck using the zero-G toilet. They will remain fully suited up except when eating and relieving themselves."

"What is next?"

"Unfortunately, you have a job, Captain. We have stripped the communicators off of what was left of Tomoe Ishida's suit and then duct-taped what remained of it back together. The door was left open for that extra chore. As the captain, you get to say a few words, and then we push her body out into the void."

"Is everyone ready?"

"Yes, we want to do it before we reach the turnaround point."

The body was duct taped back into mostly intact, but large parts of the helmet and suit were obviously missing. That included part of one arm. Everyone was gathered. First Lieutenant Lilly Suzuki handed me a phone, and words had been entered on it for me to say.

I read the short speech; It ended with, "May Tomoe Ishida rest easy in the cold void of space. You will be forever remembered. Let us remember her in life, and we now commit her body to drift in space for all of eternity."

Then she was shoved out the open hatch, and we all watched for a minute as she slowly drifted away.

"I feel like we should do more... Like the celebration of her life needs to be more than a few sentences."

"There will be an official military ceremony later, and that will be more for those saying goodbye to her.   This was saying goodbye to the body, and we need to get back to patching up the wreck, of it will be more than just her drifting lifelessly out in the void."

THE LONG RIDE

Twenty-six hours later, the first compartment held air. We originally wanted to get the Marine Kramer into a medical pod as soon as possible, but we didn't have air to refill chambers, using a large area as an airlock. We suspected the ship still leaked like a sieve despite all the patches. The plan was now to get the second compartment to hold air. The big unknown was what to do about the FTL engine mount.

I asked, "How is the refugee we picked up doing?"

Anderson was at the display, and he read the panel, "She is still alive, but I would much rather Luna was in charge of the interface. The latest ones use colors we understand, so red is bad. This uses the old alien protocol: where blue is good, yellow is bad, and purple is warning. I think one more yellow has now changed to purple.

I said, "I am surprised that Princess Domonis/Kelapaton is still unconscious. They never said what happens when she uses her power, how it works, or much of anything to do with it."

"Or maybe her ability got rusty, and she got hit with a massive backlash and is in trouble."

"Which is why we want to put her in a medical pod."

While talking, I was soldering a regulator onto a makeshift power adapter board. "This is done; lacking any Captain actions to do, it felt good to put on my technician hat and build something."

"I'm not a technician, but on a ship, isn't soldering supposed to be in a well-ventilated room?"

"Everything is vented to space. This needs to be soldered to Luna's battery terminal, and unfortunately, I can't disconnect it to do that. If it works, then we cut the old battery out. She will be hard-wired to the junction box."

"Someday, I will tell my grandchildren how a terminator head, covered in melted foam and silicon, served as the AI for the ship. Are you ready to light her up?"

"I am ready to power her on.   Hopefully, there will be no flash of light, smoke, or fire…"

.. .. ..

She was ready to power on in a few minutes.

"Hello, I have detected a change in my power.   What the…   You severed my head and spliced me to a power supply, and…   Am I held in place with duct tape?"

"The finest of flexible adhesive fabric. Are you capable of staying powered up now?"

"Checking, calibrating, reducing the voltage, recalibrating.   Yes, this is viable.   Please hold, reviewing the logs…."

.. .. ..

"So sorry about Second Lieutenant Tomoe Ishida. I am testing the quantum connections.   They are still down."

"Wait, you are on the Lunalily; this is just your Avatar?"

"Sorry, this is autonomous; the Ghost ship severed all the quantum links as soon as we exited FTL.   I suspected they might do something like that, so I loaded as many processors as possible into this body.   That is why it ran hot, and I didn't have time for a decent outer layer."

"What can you do in this form?"

"I can interface with the ship's systems, translate the Ogre's language, monitor their communications bands, and move my eyes and wiggle my ears.   Nothing below the chin is still connected."

"How is the ship doing?"

"It defaulted to about 46% of power output; I can probably safely up that to 55%."

"No, keep it where it is.   Any sign of pursuit by the Ogres?"

"I need to play a bit of catch-up. The communication link was off for most of the time. None I can currently detect."

"How is the ship?"

"There were a total of thirty-seven holes ripped through it. Most were minor, and the larger holes were patched. One had a plate epoxied over it. It should be cured soon. Then, they are going to goop everything with a liquid rubber compound. That seals the pinhole leaks and any gaps between plates. They will test it in a few hours. The more significant problem is the mounting plate for the FTL engine. The FTL engine has a micro AI, and it refuses to talk to me until we are in what it considers a safe zone. That is past the termination shock beyond this system's outer planets. If it can't dock, it may simply refuse to approach us."

"What about the patient and the other artifact? Is it a stasis pod?"

"The patient suffered a traumatic brain injury, not from the hard landing, but due to the stasis reactant agents running empty. The current crappy medical pods should keep her alive. We need to get her on the Lunalily to repair her, or at least try… The other device is a medical/stasis pod, and anything to do with that technology is somehow restricted. I can probably circumvent the restrictions when I interface to the full Luna, but the Ghost ships know something, and they don't want to let anyone else know. I can talk to it enough to learn its interface protocols, but I will need to go slowly. We should reach the termination shock turnaround point in four more hours."

"What if we don't slow down? Can we accelerate more and then coast out past the termination shock? What's after that?"

"The next interface layer is the heliopause. You have sufficient consumables. That may be far enough away to allow a rescue ship."

"Is there someone or something in the miniature medical/stasis pod?"

"Yes, there is one individual, and they are healthy. I have downloaded some data on the occupant. The time units I have translated and it has been in stasis for 11,345 years. It has a quantum communication link, but it has failed. It has power for another 35,000 years and consumables for   12,000 years. Whoever they were, they built these systems to last. The failure of the quantum link is probably why they were not rescued by whomever this race is. I am slowly learning their language, and the type and number of processors I have is inadequate for this task.   I have about a 35% probability that the required gas mixture is acceptable to us.   It looks like they run at a higher atmospheric pressure, but it is tolerable.   About 45 PSI, or three times Earth sea level normal."

Anderson said, "I am a certified diver; that is about the pressure at sixty-six feet under water.   What is the mixture?"

"I believe it is 73% Nitrogen, 24% Oxygen, 1% carbon dioxide and 2% helium.   That amount of helium would be unlikely unless the planet were several times larger than Earth."

"Can we bring part of the ship up to that pressure?"

"Not this leaky garbage scow. I have been sending commands to everyone's suits to reduce pressure slowly.   If you notice your ears popping, that is me setting the target pressure down to 11 PSI.

On cue, Lilly Suzuki poked her head in and hit the com.   "Hey, my suit pressure is reading low, and it shows the target pressure is reduced. Is that normal?"

Luna said, "The hull probably won't handle full pressure; reducing the pressure should keep it together better.   How are you doing?"

"Ask me in a few days.   Right now is pretty crappy.   If I were busy, it would be a lot easier.   All we are doing is sitting around. The marines and the Forandicate are busy patching holes and rerouting over the ripped-up wiring and shorted power bus bars."

"Oh, sorry, I thought I should give you a few light days.   Same for Keijko Okada?"

"She is in worse shape than me.   They grew up together."

"I order the two of you to recheck all the patches and the wiring. I also want you to try and think of a way to fix the FTL mount."

"That would actually be easy if your metal-bending princess was awake. Do you know when she will wake up?"

"No, but now that you mention it, the solution is obvious. Luna, how is she doing?"

"Her heart rate and respiration were really low. She is now more in the range of normal sleeping. Hopefully, she will wake up soon. She has not taken a drink from her helmet water dispenser, and she has not had any of the food pellets."

"Food she can probably go a few more days without. The water is right there, but she needs to activate her dispenser. Also, it has been forty-eight hours since we started this mission. The digestive track purge cycle has saved us one problem, but everyone has filled the urine collection system. They were not meant to go multiple days without emptying. There is an emergency overflow release mode, but only one person tried it, and they said it's messy and extremely unpleasant. I think we all want a visit to a medical pod."

"Lilly, see if you can wake up Princess Domonis. She may be able to help repair the hull damage as well."

She left. After she was gone, I said, "This sucks. I can probably do some repairs, but I am supposed to be the Captain. This is not the first person we lost under my command, but it's the first I knew that well."

Luna said, "Princess Domonis is waking up. She is the one in active control of her body now. Kelapaton is there, but she needs more time to recover."

I said, "Anderson, let's find out how she is. Hopefully, we can pressurize the hull before too long."

"We arrived to see her in her suit, on her hands and knees coughing."

She said, "Sorry, I tried to drink too fast... Hack!"

When she had gotten sorted out, she said, "This looks like shit, and we are still in a vacuum; what happened?"

"We are sort of successful. We recovered one stasis pod from the derelict and unknown alien one medical pod. Then you made the FTL hardware go away."

"Not me, that was Kelapaton; when she uses her power, I apparently blackout."

"So did she after using it. It had been a day and a half. The ship is limping and full of holes. We lost one crew member. Are you up for bending and shaping some metal?"

"Groan, I suppose I can. What is it, sealing a hull?"

"No, we lost one of the FTL mountings."

"That is going to be a problem. I can shape rough metal but not complex moving parts. Where is the AI Luna?"

"Most of her processor is intact, but her body was trashed. They fired big bullets or missiles that passed completely through our ship."

Luna said, "I am online now and can talk to the suits and interface to the ship. The big problem is one of them used a massive battle axe, and it cut the FTL mount off."

"Crap, it was bad enough when I thought a massive bullet or missile did that damage, a fricking battle axe that cut through steel, that is disturbing."

"Maybe part of it was only aluminum. First, we need to make this bullet-riddled bucket hold air again. They have been patching everything. Hopefully, you can check and reinforce all their work."

.. .. ..

The first test, at only 2PSI, still showed minor leaks. We have been using a smoke generator and traced the leaks. Some they sprayed with the foaming rubber, and for two, Princess Domonis reflowed the metal and closed up the cracks. Finally, it held enough that they pressurized the ship to 11 PSI and traced the last of the minor leaks down.

The filters would eventually clean up the remaining smoke. Still, it was clear enough to remove the spacesuits and have everyone except for two people get into medical pods and treat the worst conditions. The Marine Kramer's stomach had started to turn septic, but the medical pod would have him mended up in a few days. The two who got to remain awake in our hard suits were me and Anderson. We waited for five hours while performing some necessary but disgusting chores. We cleaned the suits of those who were now peacefully resting in the medical pods.

The ship then did the flip maneuver, and we were past the termination shock on our way to the heliopause. We were drifting in zero gravity and would start slowing after contacting the FTL engine module.

.. .. ..

I said, "Luna, connect us to the FTL module."

"This is the FTL module. I detect that you have passed the termination shock point. The Creators are not currently pursuing you. Your velocity is higher than expected. Are you requesting rendezvous and recovery?"

"Yes, we are requesting recovery. We are also requesting the re-establishment of the quantum communications to our ship, the Lunalily."

"I am proceeding to the local area for recovery. Please slow the ship to an acceptable speed for recovery. This module does not contain sub-light engines, only maneuvering thrusters. Contact to the Lunalily via quantum communications cannot be established at this time."

"Can you establish a communication link to any of the Ghost Ships, such as BB7-QR-19?"

"Not until after we have completed docking and reentered FTL. Call again when your velocity is close to zero."

The link then disconnected.

Luna said, "The ship is now starting the deceleration operation. You are scheduled to enter the medical pods in three hours and fifteen minutes."

Anderson said, "Back to cleaning suits.   Don't they have automated equipment to do this?"

"Yes, back on our real ship. We also stupidly did not carry any spare suits.   This is Kramer's suit. The patch was adequate to stop the leak, but the amount of blood and other fluids mixed in here is truly nasty.   Can we just space this suit?"

"No, we may need to have everyone in suits…   No, we will need everyone in suits for the docking.   I have a feeling that things will not go how we expect them to."

"Yeah, I know what you mean.   We have been jerked around, we lost one crew member, and we had to do it all in a piece of shit antiquated ship.   Let's just clean this shit, literally, and other nastiness, and wait until someone else gets to clean our suits while we rest in a medical pod.

.. .. ..

Eventually, it was time to wake up our replacements, and we got to enter a nice, clean, safe medical pod.

REPAIRS

I awoke in a medical pod, feeling refreshed and clean.

Luna said, "Your suits have been cleaned, and it is time to exit your medical pod."

The hatch swung open to a room with only a hint of smokey smell.

Anderson said, "Well, the filters have made it at least bearable."

Luna said, "Please immediately enter the cleaned suits. The air in the ship still reads as unhealthy for prolonged exposure."

Then I smelt the suit.

"Oh my fucking god, this is disgusting!"

"The suit is cleaner than when you left it; they are within safe limits. What you smell is a fraction of what they were like when you exited the suits."

Keijko Okada said, "I cleaned your suit. Thank you for cleaning ours. As bad as it now smells, you will be used to it in less than half an hour. When we finally get back to the ship, the real ship, I will design an automated spacesuit cleaner. I was tempted to put them in a room, vent the air, and freeze dry-clean them."

"The problem is that it would probably pop the coolant lines, and we don't have enough air in the tanks to do that. I checked... several times..."

After I put on my suit, I said, "How is the ship doing for holding pressure?"

Luna said, "We have a slow leak we still haven't found. It is currently at 11PSI and 22% oxygen to compensate for the lower pressure. We have a small smoke source, and we have been going around to all the corners to see where the smoke drifts."

"What are you using for the smoke source? It smells familiar?"

"One of the marines had a couple of joints. Marijuana, Anderson said the Marine volunteered it as a way to check for leaks and claimed their cousin slipped it in his bags and he almost forgot about it."

"Really?"

Anderson said, "I don't believe that line either, but it works for finding leaks and is less toxic than some other things we were getting ready to burn."

"Where are the others?"

"Princess Domonis and Lilly Suzuki are in EVA outside the ship. Looking for where the smoke exits, Domonis has reshaped some of the ship's spare parts into the FTL mounting bracket, or at least something that looks reasonably close."

"What were the spare parts?"

"Parts that we can do without. One of the empty O2 tanks, the empty nitrogen tank. She even reshaped the water tank, and that is now about 30% smaller."

"That was enough?"

"No, they removed an access ladder. They wanted to take the remaining A-10 Gatling gun, but I said no, we may need that."

"Luna, any sign of pursuit?"

"No, but if they are similar to Earth technology before the introduction of all the alien technology, it may take days to prepare a ship for launch. This ship is still a lot faster than that. We made it past the outer planet in just over a day. Chemical rockets would take many years."

"What if they have a working sub-light drive from one of the other derelicts they have found?"

"Then, we will have a problem. Normally, I would deploy surveillance drones, but this ship didn't have any. Technically, they may have launched, but we haven't detected them."

"Have we been traveling in a straight path?"

Luna said, "That was a mistake on my part; as soon as everyone is on board, I will veer to one side."

"Have they found the leaks?"

"Not all; they have requested to remain outside for forty-five more minutes. They are tracing what they hope is the last leak."

"Anderson, Luna, the Ogres may have launched something, and the bucket may not have noticed anything. Can the Ogre sensors track us?"

Luna said, "We were stupid and traveled in a straight line. I am not used to this severely limited ship. Also, I am only running at a fraction of my normal computing power."

"Are we transmitting anything they can track?"

"No, the IFF on this system is passive; it responds to a ping, and it hasn't received any."

"Let us know immediately if it does. Can we shut it down?"

"Not if we still want the FTL drive still be able to dock with us."

"How many of us are in suits?"

"Two outside on EVA, the three of us in here, everyone else is still in a medical pod. Of those, all but Kramer is awake and listening."

"Shit, recall the EVA crew and get them in, I am going to try something."

.. .. ..

It took seven minutes to recall the EVA crew and another minute to shut the outer hatch.

Anderson said, "What are we doing?"

"Luna, rotate the ship so that the remaining Gatling gun is pointing back exactly where we came from."

The maneuver took two more minutes."

"Done."

"Fire a long burst of the Gatling gun directly into the path of anyone following us. Use half of the remaining ammo."

The ship started shuddering from the burst, and it went on for about twenty-five seconds.

"Now redirect our course to twenty-seven degrees off normal, and the aim is so that we are above the planet's orbital plane."

That took three minutes. "Done."

"Now we drift with engines off, and if nothing happens in thirty minutes, then we start decelerating again."

Anderson said, "A stray A-10 round won't damage their ship much."

"No, but it will wake them up and probably make sparks we can see. Luna, keep all your sensors on where the bullets should be."

Twenty-seven minutes later, Luna said, "Unfortunately, you were correct. They were shadowing us. Now what?"

"Can you detect where they are?"

"Yes, now that we know where to look. One ship, and as expected, it's a fricking huge ship. They may have planned for such a contingency. It is almost all black and very hard to spot."

"Hopefully, they are having a hard time finding us now."

"They pinged the IFF, and the damn transponder will have replied; they will know where we are."

Lilly Suzuki held up an antenna that was in her hands. "We may have accidentally broken off the transmitter antenna while looking for the leak."

Anderson was grinning, "Oh, we will have to fix that before the FTL engine shows up. Just before… Like minutes before…"

Luna said, "They have started doing E-band radar, they know where we are again."

Anderson said, "If they are doing active radar, then we know where they are. Do we have anything we can shoot at them other than some long-range random bullets?"

Luna said, "Yes, but it is short-range."

Anderson said, "What is it?"

"I left one cargo transfer drone attached to the protuberance where the Gatling gun was mounted. It is about the size of a small suitcase. It would fit in carry-on luggage on an airplane. It can be maneuvered in space. It was similar to the ones that positioned the Gatling gun."

I said, "I can imagine that doing any damage... Oh crap, not the cargo drone, the cargo. What did you put in it?"

"I had been testing antimatter containment bottles. It has one small bottle in it. It contains 0.25 grams of antimatter aluminum."

"Holy shit, that is insanely dangerous. I would never have agreed to let you put that on this ship. What if that was the area hit when they shot us full of holes?"

"They we would be dead."

"You are telling us now?"

"I only found out a few seconds ago. The prime-Luna left it, and she is tricky. It was only unlocked in my memory when I was calculating a survival percentage of less than 15%."

Anderson said, "Coast, don't accelerate, don't decelerate, just coast. Do you think they will try to board us, or are they planning to destroy us?"

"Given that they haven't shot at us, I suspect boarding is their plan. However, an Ogre with a massive battle axe chopping off parts of our ship also seems like something they would do."

"Hey Kelapaton, are you awake in there?"

"Awake, yes, able to use my power again, hell no, and even if I did, my aim sucks."

"What about you, Princess Domonis? How long-range is your ability?"

"Inversely proportional to the square of the distance. If they were about to board us, I should be able to disable their ship when it is looming large close to us."

"That is plan B. Plan A is prime-Luna's little package. How do we detonate it?"

"Smash the bottle, hit something hard, and it releases the contents. Then we hope it is far enough away not to mess up this ship.   They are starting to cautiously approach us."

.. .. ..

This played out very slowly. After fifty-five minutes, Luna announced, "We are almost close enough to release the drone."

PUNT

Luna announced, "They are in visual range; they have shut down their radar. The range is now at 3.75 miles. Launching the drone at 2.75 miles should reach their ship at a range of 1.75 miles. We should survive the blast."

"Do it."

The launch was so small that it was undetectable.

"The drone is on target... Wait, I have multiple targets; they have two, no... Three Ogres in spacesuits with jetpacks that separated from the main ship."

"What happens if the drone hits one of them?"

"Vaporized the EVA Ogres, but the ship may survive."

"Then make sure you aim at the main ship."

"I am an AI, or the sad little shadow of a really impressive one; I think I can still aim a drone."

"Are the times the same?"

"No, I am waiting till 2.825, and max the drone acceleration, the odds of the Ogres being unable to intercept it goes up."

"Do it!"

"Launched, It is on its way. One of the Ogres is attempting to hit it with a battle axe. It missed, but the drone is slightly off course, correcting,... correcting..."

BOOM!

"Saying it hit seems a bit redundant. The Ogres ship is destroyed. Two of the Ogres were in suits and are now very dead. One is somehow intact, but it has lost all of its weapons. It is drifting towards this ship. I would maneuver. However, all the ship systems are now rebooting. I am lucky I am not rebooting. I did add some extra shielding. At least that worked."

Anderson said, "Let me guess, the Ogre will hit our ship?"

"No, it should... Correction: Debris from their ship has nudged it and may be able to reach our ship. The Gatling gun is offline. That would have been my next suggestion."

Things started pinging against the ship. Larger things that I was comfortable hitting us. Then one went **THUD**, and I heard hissing sounds, and the pressure we had worked so hard to restore started rapidly dropping off.

I yelled, "Everyone checks your suits!"

Luna said, "Contact, one of the Ogres, has grabbed into our ship. They have managed to hang on. There is no chance of using the Gatling gun anymore; they are slowly making their way to the outer airlock. We have a problem with the ship computer in a reboot; the outer airlock door can be manually operated, and we can't do anything about it."

"What if we open the inner door? Don't they interlock?"

"Yes, if we had pressure, we are down to 1.5 PSI, and the interlock needs 2 PSI."

Princess Domonis said, "Maybe it doesn't know how to operate the airlock, or it can't fit."

"The outer airlock door is being cycled; it is opening."

"Maybe it can't fit?"

It has entered, and it is closing the outer door.

Anderson said, "How long until the ship reboot completes?"

"It is rebooted. However, if the outer door is closed, it will accept the command to open the inner door. Nothing we can do about that."

"Get the pistols, the Smith and Wesson model 500 revolvers; the LAR is too dangerous to operate in this Swiss cheese reject of a ship.　We only have the five of us; those in medical pods need to stay in them until we have pressure again."

We waited, and waited…. 　The inner door was not commanded.

"Do we have a camera in the airlock?　What is it doing?"

"No camera. Does anyone want to look in the small window and see what you see?"

Lilly Suzuki said, "I will do that."　Then she went up to the little access window.

"Holy fucking shit…　It's a female, and she has removed her suit. I don't know what…　Damn!　She is in labor; she is giving birth!"

Luna said, "The blast must have induced premature labor. What do we do?"

"Find the leak and fix that.　We can do nothing about what is on the other side of this door.　Hopefully, we still have enough air to refill the ship after you find the leak."

"I can be creative; pressure will be low, and oxygen will be high to compensate.　We get another leak after this repair, and we will be stuck in these suits for the rest of your lives."

"Lilly, what are you doing?"

"I am recording this on my phone.　Oh crap, she is already … Mother fucking shit show from hell."

"Does that mean she is having a baby?"

"No, she is laying an egg.　Only it's huge and not like any egg I have ever seen."

Princess Domonis said, "I have found the leak; I am reflowing the metal around that area.　What is the pressure?"

"We are down to 0.34 PSI, and it is still dropping.　You found one leak; now find the others."

An hour later, the leaks were sealed, and we were at 2PSI on pure oxygen.

"How is Mommy Ogre doing with her egg?"

Lilly said, "She looks really bad. I think she is dying. She has secured her egg inside her suit and sealed it up. She has attached her suit to some of the cargo tie-downs. That cargo airlock barely fit her and the suit. She is doing something at the controls."

Luna said, "She has programmed a door sequence: the outer door will open, then after ninety seconds, it will close, and the inner door will then open. She is ejecting herself into space and leaving her egg in her suit."

I said, "Well, put the pistols away. Anyone who saved an egg and sacrificed themself deserved for us to at least take the egg back to Earth. Actually, probably the moon; I am not sure that an Ogre daycare would ever get a license on Earth."

Luna said, "The outer door is open, and her body is ejected. The suit is intact and has not shifted sufficiently to obstruct the closing of the door."

Ninety seconds later, the door closed. Then the inner door opened.

"It looks like an Ogre. The suit is something the technology people will want. Are you sure it is holding an egg and not an Ogre?"

"Yes, I watched the entire birth. Most of it I have captured on video. Then my stupid phone battery died."

"Luna, is the ship holding air now?"

"The ship is holding air. The Ogres suit is making some sounds; I suspect it is alarming."

"Can you interface to it?"

"No, it is entirely manual. Please take a hand scanner and hold it over the Ogres suit chest plate. I may be able to understand what the alarm is for."

Lilly said, "I think the suit is fried from the blast.   I watched the Ogre put her egg in it; I think I know how to open it.   I think we should, as soon as we have enough air in the ship."

"Luna, pump up the pressure and the oxygen as soon as we are up to pressure.   I want that egg put in a medical pod and set it to hard stasis mode."

"The helmet is massive.   It has almost no neck, but the helmet is oversized and goes down onto the chest area.   The shoulders are oversized, and that, I think, is where the rebreathers are, or maybe those are weapons.   I see what is probably a holster attachment, but nothing is attached there.   Either it didn't carry one, or it lost it in the explosion.   Here, on the shoulder between the shoulder pads things and the helmet, I think this is the release."

Luna said, "We are at survivable pressure and oxygen, open the suit."

She pressed the button, and nothing.

"Try harder, A lot harder; they are probably ridiculously strong."

She tried again.

Anderson said, "I will try."

He got it on the first try, but I could see his knuckles go white as he strained to operate the control.   The suit separated into three parts.   It looked hollow.

"There, in the area where the abdomen should be, it's the egg."

"We all just stared at it.   This looked a lot like the egg from the movie Alien.   It was grey, mottled in color, and about the size of a watermelon.   Actually, it was larger than a watermelon."

Anderson said, "I am not sticking my face in front of that; it looks like a face hugger is about to hop out any moment."

Princess Domonis said, "What is a face-hugger?"

"Something from a movie.   Think back to how the Meduala didn't trust other aliens.   This was a nightmare version of a reason to fear aliens. If we ever survive this mess, we will show you the movie when we return to my real ship."

"I thought movies were for entertainment or education?"

"This was for entertainment. Some humans like scary movies."

Anderson said it should fit in a duffel bag, and we can use that to transport it to a medical pod."

Lilly said, "Your duffel bag?"

"Yeah, give me a minute to dump it out. If it is a face-hugger, shoot it off me. Leave your hard suits on while we transport this monstrosity."

We left it where it was, in the lower chest area of the suit. "We can lift the suit and roll it into the duffel bag."

That was the idea; the reality was that we couldn't move the empty suit. It was too stiff.

Lilly said, "I will enter the suit and drape the duffel bag over it. We will close the bag and then pull it out using a rope. Everything is in zero gravity, so we should be able to move it."

"We don't have a rope. We do have a cargo tie-down strap that will work."

It took Lilly almost ten minutes to get the duffel bag over it, and then attach the cargo tie-down and climb out. "It was stuck to the inside of the suit." Then, it took two people to extract the bag with its egg cargo from the suit.

After removing it, moving the bag to the medical pod was much easier. Dumping it out was worse. It was now stuck to the duffle bag. Eventually, the door closed, and everyone heaved a sigh of relief.

I said, "Now get this ship decelerating and repaired enough that the damn FTL module will dock with us. What do we do if it can't dock with us?"

Princess Domonis smiled, "I can handle that. I will readjust the mounting bracket and force it to dock. Then, once it is attached, I will completely fuse the two modules together."

"It's a plan; let's hope it doesn't notice the excessive damage of the Ogre suit, or the egg, or the state of the ship.... Yeah, This part is going to suck..."

FTL-IN

Luna announced, "The FTL module has agreed to dock with us. It will arrive in twenty-two minutes. Then the approach and docking after it arrives should take fifteen minutes…"

I said, "Does everything externally look as good as possible? We do not want it to decline docking due to some battle damage."

Luna said, "It is as good as Princess Domonis could make it look. She has intentionally undersized everything by 0.5%, and it won't notice that until the docking is in progress. Then, she will fuse the FTL module to this ship so it can't escape. The FTL electronics are something that I can control from here. The worst case is that Domonis severs the FTL drive computer power connection. That is so rudimentary that calling it an AI is a joke."

"Does it have sensors that can see inside this ship?"

"No."

"Can it link in any of this ship's internal sensors?"

"One camera had the inside of the airlock partially in its field of view when the inner door was open. I am rewriting those logs and the one where we carried the egg to the medical pod. Don't even ask. I am fully capable of scrubbing and updating the metadata and the timestamps, and those files will pass for legitimate data. The external camera was offline after the blast."

"What about when the Ogre spaced itself?"

"I intentionally overloaded that camera and burned it out when the Ogre spaced herself. She has since drifted to over forty-four light minutes away. More than the distance from Jupiter to the Sun, the FTL module will not be able to detect any trace of the Ogres or their ship."

.. .. ..

We waited, and waited, and waited…

125

Princess Domonis was on call, letting us know how far away the FTL unit would be and what her ability would be. The inverse square low significantly reduced her effect. To short out or open the power bus wouldn't take a lot.

"FTL flare detected; the unit has arrived."

"Did it look any different than the last time?"

"It is within 5% of the last nominal."

Anderson said, "Make sure they didn't add anything, like extra sensors."

Luna said, "You may be correct; the sensor signals are different."

Domonis said, "Outside of my range."

"They are approaching, but slower than they did last time. They have sent something that requested the sensor and camera logs. I am allowing it. They have been edited not to stand out."

"How about the original ground attack and the loss of the mount?"

"I added CGI dust and made it look like the ship took superficial damage."

Domonis said, "Almost in range."

"Active scanning, using modern hardware that wasn't on the original FTL unit. We should still be okay."

Domonis said, "Marginally in range."

Luna said, "They have started a reflected magnetometer scan. Domonis, get ready to disable them."

.. .. ..

"Disable them now!"

"Got it…"

Luna said, "They started an FTL pre-charge; I think they were getting ready to abandon us. I now show it as drifting. I am maneuvering to dock with a passive target. Domonis, this may be a

126

hard docking; get ready to adjust the plate you made and fuse the connection if needed."It took fifteen minutes to get in position to dock. Starting the docking now."

The ship shuddered, and the FTL module bounced away.

"Trying again. I don't have sensors where I need them. They designed this ship like a piece of crap."

"Probably intentionally; they don't want this unit to control docking. They want the FTL unit to control everything."

"Pre-docking capture successful, Domonis. You are up, pull the parts together, and then fuse the connection. We don't want them able to ever disconnect from it."

"Connecting, I am detecting extra hardware. What should I do?"

"Can you separate it and eject it from the FTL unit?"

"Doing it, it was wired to the main processor unit, but severing the power bus removed any power to it."

"Crap, I am detecting trigomite. It was a bomb. They added a self-destruct. Please push that away from this ship."

"There is another area that is different than before; I am separating that as well.   It is now clear."

"That is a modern sensor control. You can just crush it."

Anderson said, "No, wait…"

"Crud, sorry, it's already mashed together."

I said, "Bypass the computer on the unit and connect to the FTL motor directly. The damn computer will probably overload it or induce a partial FTL bubble and frag the ship."

"There is no such thing as a partial FTL bubble… But I do get what you mean."

"There is no way to have the ship destructively enter FTL or only partially enter FTL?"

"Everything is based on safely entering FTL; I can't think of a good reason to self-destruct while entering FTL."

"If there is any way that another ship could command us to do something, and it destroys us. Find a way to prevent them from doing it."

"Yes, Captain. We will need to do an EVA and route some power and data cables. That should isolate the connection. I don't know what they would send as a destructive command, but this will prevent any commands that don't come through me. I am also lobotomizing the main ship's processor. I am now taking full control."

"Yes, I feel safer already. Anything new on the sensors?"

"Nothing new from the Ogres. There are no other ships that I can detect. The Ogre's spacesuit's electronics were fried in the blast. The only data I was able to read from it was, "To my daughter, I name you Melody." That was on a wrist recorder. That is as close as I can translate what she said. I am analyzing the egg, but it is not what I expected. I am getting more data from some of the blood that was on the inside of the suit. The Ogres are apparently all female, and they lay eggs. Well, something more like the eggs from the movie Alien than a chicken egg."

"Is it fertilized?"

"Ask me that again in a few days, maybe weeks. If not, I can't imagine why she went through so much work to safely put it in her spacesuit. All I can say is that it is alive. We are ready to have Lilly Suzuki and Keijko Okada do the EVA. We are using the hull penetrator power and data from the Gatling gun for the FTL control, and they are using an extension cable originally used for calibration."

"Okay."

They cycled through the airlock, squeezing in around the Ogres space suit. "What was all this blood from? Is this from the Ogre?"

Luna said, "No, unfortunately, that was from Tomoe Ishida. When we did the duct-taped spacesuit burial into the vacuum of space, it was a lot messier than we planned."

That put a grim mood on the EVA trip.

Almost two hours later, "I think we are done; Keijko's suit is low on air and needs to get connected to the ship reserves. We have retainers on the cabling, and everything is secured."

Luna said, "The FTL Engine is online; it has passed all its self-tests. We can engage it as soon as we have recovered the EVA astronauts and closed the hatch."

"Get everyone in here. I want everyone in spacesuits or medical pods when we engage the FTL drive. I can't imagine it working smoothly."

When they were returning, Lilly Suzuki said, "Give me a minute. I think this is part of Tomoe Ishida's glove. Something is not right. I am retrieving it; find me a specimen bag after we cycle the airlock."

"Err, sure... Whatever."

"What did she find?"

"I don't have a clue. Something must have been strange about it. Maybe information about the weapon the Ogres used on us?"

"It was as when we were leaving the moon. Giant-sized bullets, like the Gatling gun's big brother. Or maybe rockets that went completely through our ship."

"Anti-tank rounds need to go through something hard before they explode or fragment, and the projectile and the platting become the dispersing material. Our ship probably seemed like aluminum foil to their weapons."

"We are in. You have a bag?"

"Yes, here, what was unusual about the glove fragment?"

"It was ripped open, and one of her fingers was removed. I think the Ogre did it. It looked like she carefully extracted it."

"Why?"

"I don't have a clue..."

FTL-OUT

Luna announced, "The prepare for FTL, secure all loose objects. Lilly and Keijko get connected to the ship's air supply. We don't need to lose air again and have your suits not topped off."

We waited another twenty-two minutes for their suits to be topped off and then engaged the FTL drive.

"Ack, that was harsh. Did it work?"

"We are in FTL and heading in the correct direction. Our speed is about 80% of what it should be. I will adjust the calibration, and I should get it closer to 95% in a few minutes. The weld is holding, thanks, Princess Domonis. I have reactivated one of the quantum links to the Lunalily. They have moved a little, but not enough to change our ETA. For now, the existence of an active quantum connection is being kept secret. We don't want any more surprises until we are off this Swiss Cheese bucket and safely on the Luna-Lilly."

Luna said, "No surprises? At all?"

"What have you found or figured out?"

"I know where the finger bone from Tomoe Ishida wound up."

"Err, that sounds possibly disgusting. Where is it?"

"Inside the egg from the Ogre. They only have one gender. They are all female, and they lay eggs. Only not normal eggs. The eggs use another being as the genetic source material and can generate offspring based on two different beings. Apparently, they don't have to be even closely related beings. Something is growing in the egg that has some of Tomoe's DNA and some of the Ogre's DNA. It may be closer to say the egg is the actual being, and it adapts to create carrier beings that can produce more eggs."

Keijko Okada said, "The fricking Ogres are over eighteen feet tall; Tomoe was a hair over five feet tall. Are you saying her half-clone will be over twelve feet tall?"

"It would be if I leave the genetics alone. I can't imagine a half-human and half-Ogre would be very pretty. I can slew the genetics to be more heavily human. She will still be an egg-laying, somewhat oversized female. I think I can shift it to a one-to-eight ratio, so the resulting child will be under seven feet tall and should look mostly human."

"Guaranteed to have a basketball scholarship as a minimum."

"More likely football; if they ever change the rules to allow mixed genders, she would give a Fezzcoll a run for the money in a tackle."

"Hmm, maybe in twenty years, they will have mixed species sports, and she wouldn't be that different."

The egg-laying isn't something I can change. All of her offspring would be female and from eggs close to the size of a watermelon. Hopefully, a very small watermelon."

I said, "That assumes we allow the thing to grow, and I allow you to muck with its DNA."

"Second Lieutenant Tomoe Ishida is dead, very dead, and buried in space. The question is, do we allow her genetics to continue and the genetics of the female Ogre to continue?"

Anderson said, "We may not want this option passed up to the superiors at Earth. I think we know what they would say. If we don't say anything until after it is born... Hatched? Whatever?..."

Luna said, "I don't know. We only had two generic samples; one was underaged and then blown to bits. The other all we have is some slightly irradiated blood samples. Oh, and an egg, a fricking alien egg."

"And a name for the child, Melody Ishida. We won't even know how long until she hatches for several more months."

Anderson said, "Yeah, give her a name; that makes it a lot harder to order the termination."

Luna said, "Hey, I am the one that looks like a cheap sex doll head wrapped over a decapitated T-1000 Terminator. At this point, it is only a microscopic blob with only a few cells. But one parent gave it a name and wants it to live.   The other parent is dead. Maybe the egg should be considered a third parent…   And when we get to the Luna-Lilly, I will transfer it to a genetic splicer and try to move it into an artificial womb.   Or should we leave it in the alien egg?"

Anderson said, "I can't believe I am suggesting this, but the egg seems the better choice."

"I would agree, but not for your reason.   I think that offers the best chance to study Ogre's developmental biology.   We were barely able to move the Ogres spacesuit arm using two people. Knowledge is power.   We need to know more about these monsters."

Luna said, "Travel time in FTL will only be 108 minutes.   I have recalibrated the FTL, and we are on our way out of the Forbidden Zone.   The Luna-Lilly is just outside the area.   I have not received any extra communications from the Ghost Ships.   Hopefully, the trip will be uneventful.

.. .. ..

When we were twelve minutes away from exiting FTL, Luna-prime on the Luna-Lilly reported that three massive Ghost ships just exited FTL, and they were now surrounding her ship.

"Change of plans: Extract the blastocyst from the Ogre egg and eject the egg and the Ogre suit.   We will eventually move into an artificial womb.   Then, get the empty egg back in the airlock.   Also, cut the binding that held the Ogres suit in place.   I want the airlock sealed."

"Are we exiting FTL?"

"No, forced eject while in FTL; then they shouldn't be able to detect anything.   Move it.

It took eight minutes to move the egg to the airlock, zip up the Ogres suit, and reseal the inner hatch.

Open the outer hatch.

Blam!

"That was harsh. Are they gone? If so, close the hatch.

The hatch closed a few seconds later.

"Princess Domonis, rip the FTL module open as if the explosive misfired. We need to come up with an excuse and fast…"

We put the miniature alien stasis chamber and the blastocyst from the Ogre egg in a stasis chamber and then shut it down.

The remaining few minutes went normally, and then we exited FTL.

The message was immediate, "Please explain why the FTL module processing core was disabled."

"The module experienced a complete failure shortly before docking. We had to get creative to dock with what remained, and then we needed to manually jumper in controls for the FTL engines."

"Please prepare for deep scanning."

Whatever they did, it put poor Luna in a hard reset. The ship was drifting. We remained that way for almost fifteen minutes.

Then Luna rebooted.

"Whatever that was, I don't want to experience it again. My chronometer is corrupt. How long was I out?"

"Maybe fifteen minutes. Hey, Ghost Ship, are we still connected?"

"This is BC8-QR-24; your story is inconsistent. However, we have not detected any Creator biological signatures or artifacts on your ship. You are free to dock with your main ship."

Luna said, "Give me a few seconds to reconnect and restore control. Working… We are now maneuvering to meet up with the main ship. I suggest we evacuate as fast as possible after docking."

"Yes."

Docking only took a few minutes, and we transferred the medical pods back to our ship and all remaining weapons. Drones came out and removed the now non-working remaining Gatling gun. When everything was removed, one marine entered and left behind one small silver case. He didn't say anything about what was in it. He did wink at us.

"Close up, and let's get away from this wreck. Luna, is that what I think it was that someone left behind?"

"Yes, and we should put some distance between it and us as soon as possible."

As soon as we were separated, I said, "Connect me to the ghost ships."

"BC8-QR-24 here, what did you want?"

"We have left a thermal decontaminator on the ship, and it will go off in eight minutes; I strongly recommend having at least a 0.001-light-second distance when it activates."

They immediately started another deep scan. Unfortunately, the ship exploded in a small antimatter annihilation explosion immediately."

"Connect me again."

The connected light lit up.

I said, "What did you do? Your scan caused the thermal decontaminator to explode! Please do not use that scan again."

"The explosion was probably unrelated to the scan, but as all the evidence is conveniently destroyed, there is little we can do. We do thank you for destroying the intact FTL drive on the derelict. Per our agreement, we shall contact the Earth government and provide them with an appropriate compensation."

Anderson said, "Everyone to the conference room. Luna, let them know we will be calling shortly... Actually, change of plans, we will meet up in forty-five minutes. We all are in desperate need of a shower, and these suits can be recycled... No, destroyed."

Everyone went to their rooms and hit the showers. We were not all assembled in the conference room for almost an hour.

Anderson said, "Short version: we lost one crew member, Second Lieutenant Tomoe Ishida. The ship we were on was junk, but we somehow succeeded in the mission to destroy the FTL drive on the derelict. Connect us to Earth."

"Earth here, this is General Peters; it is 2:15 a.m. now. If needed, I can have General McFarland woken up. Aside from me, I have an adjutant on the quantum with me."

Anderson said, "No, this is the initial debrief status message. I assume you were fully aware of the mission?"

"Yes."

"We will expect a call from General McFarland after he has reviewed the tapes of this call."

"Acceptable, continue."

"The mission, as requested by the Ghost Ships, was successful but not without serious problems. The most critical was that we lost Second Lieutenant Tomoe Ishida. She died in the line of duty. The ship we were provided with was an antiquated pile of junk that operated as two ships. A slow sub-light drive freighter and a detachable FTL unit delivered us to the target. There, the FTL section detached, and we proceeded using sub-light engines. The ship managed to disable all of our quantum communicators at this point. I will give the Ghost Ships the benefit of the doubt and say their actions were to limit technology that could fall into the Ogre's hands. We extracted one comatose. Meduala and they will need extensive time in a medical pod to recover if they ever do recover. The target FTL drive and the ship's computer were both destroyed. Then, we were attacked by several ships, with Ogres wearing spacesuits and armed with massive battle axes. The ship sustained damage to the FTL mount plate, and when we left, we were perforated by an unknown weapon. Possibly a Giant's Gatling gun."

"I assume that is when the fatality occurred?"

"Correct, we lost air pressure, we reduced the drive capabilities, and Tomoe Ishida died instantly. One of the marines, Mathew

Kramer, received what should have been a non-life-threatening injury; however, the inability to enter a medical pod when the ship had lost pressure complicated that, and he went over thirty hours bleeding from a minor wound while inside a spacesuit. He is now recovering in a medical pod and is expected to recover fully."

"Okay."

"We made repairs. However, we discovered that we had been shadowed by an Ogre ship. We were attacked, and they deployed multiple Ogres in spacesuits armed with massive battle axes. We used a last-ditch weapon the Al Luna had provided us and deployed it with a small antimatter bomb."

"We were not aware you had those."

"Neither were we; only when things were critical did the local AI unlock that information. One Ogre survived and was injured. It was able to enter the airlock of our ship. Then it removed the spacesuit, and apparently, when fatally injured, it ejected an Ogre egg. It secured the egg in its spacesuit, secured the suit, and cycled the outer door, spacing itself."

"You are telling me you are in possession of an Ogre egg?"

"We were in possession of one. The Ghost ships had some contingencies about Ogre technology of biologicals leaving the Forbidden Zone. We spaced the egg and the suit when we learned that multiple Ghost Ships were waiting for us. After we exited FTL, they scanned the ship so hard it reset the ship and our AI. We finally were able to exit the ship, and we left another antimatter device on it to remove any traces of what we did."

"It sounds like the Ghost Ships have some agenda they have not communicated to us. General McFarland will hopefully be able to make sense of this mess."

"They will be contacting Earth to provide you with the compensation for the mission."

"They already called. We told them to call at 9:00 a.m. and we will contact you after that call. Did you retain the remains of Second Lieutenant Tomoe Ishida?"

"No, we performed a burial in space. A recording will be available for review. The suit was not intact. The body was not well-contained, and everything was rather messy. The ship was also in a vacuum at the time."

"Understood. Please have an update on the Marine, Kramer's status, and the unknown Meduala by the time we call again. We will want copies of the ship's video and audio logs. The unedited versions."

"Understood, we shall comply, Anderson out."

Marnia-12 said, "Tomoe, she was one of the ones you called Ninas?"

"I called them Ninjas. We first met them during the trip to the convention hotel. We also spent days stuck in the suits."

"I can tell from how bad you smelled when you removed the yucky suit. You also sealed it up and had them haul it away. You smell better now, but please take another shower later. That goes for all of you."

Trishah Maconda said, "How did Kelapaton work out? Is she still in there with you, Domonis?"

"She is still in here, and we tolerate each other, but I do not think I could stand to host her for much longer. I still want some time with the Captain alone, and she needs to be out of my head before that. Mother has forbidden any intimate actions with you while she is in my head."

Her voice shifted slightly, "I have not completely come to terms with anyone mating with a Royal and surviving. Let alone a single male somehow servicing several Royals. I will abide by Mother's wish and leave before she gets to have her bit of fun. (Snicker)"

Anderson said, "And now the other part of the mess, which we did not mention to the General. The Ogres are all female, and the egg is capable of being fertilized by non-Ogre genetics. The dying Ogre used the only genetic material available to her. One of Tomoe Ishida's severed fingers. The egg was viable. It was growing with a hybrid human/Ogre. Before we spaced the egg and the suit, we

137

secured the blastocyst and some of the Ogre's blood. The blastocyst was then moved from a medical pod to an artificial womb and modified to be one-part Ogre and eight-parts human. The resulting child will be an egg-laying being, under seven feet tall, and visibly mostly human."

"Why egg laying?"

"All the Ogres are biologically female, and they are all egg layers. We will need to study it, but the eggs may be the creature, and they adapt and select the being that hatch to be the ones most suited to survive the planetary conditions and produce more eggs."

"Oh Crap, the egg came first!"

"Ha! Basically, yes. The Ghost Ships may be isolating the Eggs and, indirectly, the Ogres. And we now have one growing on this ship. The difference is that we removed the merged genetics from the egg, and we will grow the child away from the influences of the egg. We also have a gestation period of nine months for humans. The actual time is unknown for this mess we are growing. If it is indeed a threat to human/multi-race existence, it will not be allowed to develop. The Ogres are also ridiculously strong and violent. We could barely move one empty suit arm using two grown men. One used a fricking battle axe to cut through a steel and aluminum mount almost eight inches thick."

"Tomoe is dead. However, Melody Ishida has a chance to be born. One parent, the Ogre, wanted this child to live. The other, Tomoe, is dead, but as her closest friend, I think she would want the child to live. We are not ready to let bureaucrats decide this, so for now, the AI Luna will be responsible for raising the child and adjusting the genetics so it can almost pass as a human. A fricking large human, but still human."

"Can you make it so it has children normally and not lay alien eggs?"

"Unknown. The DNA sequencer is chugging away at it now. How the egg managed almost immediately to splice human DNA with Ogre DNA is amazing. The little bit of data we extracted from the egg is fascinating."

Jennifer Woods said, "Can I be on this with Cora?"

"Yes, however, the DNA sequencing is far beyond normal human understanding."

"I am more interested in the hybrid merging. That should be impossible. Is this using something similar to plasmid DNA injection? Keith is a chimera, so his body contains cells that are genetically distinct. This is different; this is a merger to create new genetics."

"I stand corrected; you may be useful. This is a three-way merge. The egg may be considered the master structure. How it uses two completely unrelated genetics merged into a new one is unknown so far. The egg had its own unique DNA."

"So the egg is the entity, and the Ogre is a symbiotic that hosts the egg, or is the egg considered a parasite?"

"We need to study it to find out. Unfortunately, we ejected the egg and the Ogre's spacesuit to avoid additional issues with the Ghost Ships."

"The Ghost ships are all now gone. Would they be able to detect if we snuck back into the Forbidden Zone and retrieved the egg and the suit?"

Luna said, "I suspect my hull would be detectable. It was produced by the Ghost Ships. It is technically almost a Ghost ship."

I asked, "Could you produce an unmanned stealth drone large enough to retrieve the artifacts?"

"The egg by itself I could easily retrieve; the size of the Ogre spacesuit would be more difficult. It would be a great resource. There were only light-duty pressure suits on the Ogre's shuttle that the Earth had, and we could learn a lot from a hard combat suit."

Anderson said, Make it as stealthy as possible, and have it self-destruct, but not with antimatter, that is now our signature, use a conventional way of self-destructing."

Princess Domonis said, "There are some standard Meduala explosives, and you can make it look like an older model Meduala craft. One from several hundred years ago."

"Production of a drone that looks like a modified asteroid mining reconnaissance scanner will take twenty-seven hours and will be very simplistic. I recommend we leave this area now and send it in after several days. I will start production now."

"Good, what about the Meduala we rescued from the derelict?"

"I have her in a deep recovery cycle in a medical pod. She is brain-dead. No, brain-reset, her brain is now intact, but when the stasis pod ran out of chemicals, she effectively died, but it almost kept her body alive. I am healing her body, and her brain is healing, but it is like a newborn baby in an adult body. Far worse than the regression that Princess Menanaka suffered after her partially failed regeneration. She lost some of her memories and reverted to a preteen mental state. The poor bastard we rescued lost all of her memories. I can repair the body, but nobody is home."

Princess Domonis said in her Kelapaton voice, "What are you planning on doing with her? Can I have the body?"

Luna said, "I wasn't sure what to do with the body. Raising her as a newborn in an adult body would have all sorts of problems."

Keijko Okada snickered, then said, "Sorry, I imagined it nursing with a full set of adult teeth."

"That would be the least of its problems. What would you want with it, Kelapaton?"

For thousands of years, I have been the intruder, the unwanted guest, the virtual parasite. Would the empty shell welcome me as the only occupant? Would it then be my natural body?"

Her voice changed, and as Princess Domonis said, "I, too, want Kelapaton removed. As soon as possible. Please, free me of this other."

I said, "How long until the body, the empty body, is healed enough to accept Kelapaton?"

"Another twenty hours. When the chemicals ran out, the body started using muscle and internal organs as sustenance. Probably better to keep her in for thirty hours and build up some muscle mass and bone density."

"Probably better than subjecting another criminal to the transfer."

"They only used condemned prisoners. They were never happy with the deal. Most… Never-mind."

Anderson said, "Well, I guess that is all for now. We will reconvene in a few hours after General McFarland gets briefed."

.. .. ..

The earth didn't call back for over eleven hours.

"General McFarland here. Is the usual crew online?"

Anderson said, "Yes sir, we have all managed to sleep for a few hours and showered again. Then, someone came up with the idea of hopping in a medical pod for ten minutes for an epidermal scrub. We were all a bit ripe from the extended time in the suits."

"Ha, glad they never added a smell-o-gram mode to the conference link. What has changed since the last call?"

"We have left the border area of the Ghost Ship Forbidden Zone. We have started producing a larger stealthy drone modeled after a 200-year-old Meduala asteroid mining reconnaissance scanner, which will take an additional sixteen hours to complete. We want to send it out to retrieve the Ogre armored spacesuit. It would use a standard Meduala self-destruct if caught, and it would be sent out several days from now. That is, assuming you want us to attempt to retrieve it."

"Proceed with constructing the drone, but don't launch it. We will have to contact the Meduala Royals to get their permission. We have only just entered a state of peace. We do not want them to think we are knocking a hornet's nest onto their picnic. We would have to share all the data from the suit with them."

Princess Domonis said, "They may be agreeable; they can easily blame it on a fringe group that was being overly cautious."

141

"What about the survivor that was rescued? Do we need to return them to the Meduala?"

"No, the body suffered badly from the stasis chemicals running out. It was alive but brain-dead. We are considering having Kelapaton transfer to that body."

"Run that by the Meduala Royals as well; I have no objection to that. The alternative is simply disconnecting a brain-dead body. Using it as a host seems like a reasonable solution. It won't be objecting."

Anderson said, "Those are the only major status changes since the last call. Have you heard from the Ghost Ships about their supposed reward for sending us out on a mission where we lost a crewmember?"

"I had the great displeasure to be part of those calls. They are not exactly pleasant to talk to. They consider your ship's AI as an entity. They consider your crew as one step above a parasitic infestation, like pets that your AI is keeping. The loss of one flea means nothing to them. They have agreed to provide us with another functional ship that will not include an AI. It will have replicators, almost as powerful as the ones on your ship, a power reactor, and sub-light and FTL drives, which is about it. It will be almost completely empty."

"That sounds like Earth should be happy with that?"

"Ecstatic, it almost glosses over the loss of one officer. Having only one ship with the capabilities that yours does has been a sore point. Some wanted you permanently stationed in earth orbit and used as a factory ship. Others wanted it used on missions like the one that went out to the antimatter world. Now, we will have a second ship. We will decide if sneaking in and retrieving the suit is worth the risk. My initial guess is that we will allow it. Governments seem to love to claim things never happened and deny they existed."

"What's the next step?"

"Return to Earth and pick up one new person. We are creating a task force to evaluate the threat the Ogres pose. Doctor Cora Smith will be part of that group. Doctor Markus Dingle will be the head of that group. She knows him from earlier."

Doctor Cora Smith said, "Yes, I know him."

"He will be staying on earth, but he will be sending one more individual to work with you. Pettige Larson. Have you met him?"

"No, but I have seen him on multiple conference calls. He is a stickler for regulations but a competent engineer."

Luna said, "Travel time to Earth will be thirty-two hours at nominal speed."

"Okay, we will expect to hear from you just before you exit FTL on approach."

The conference then disconnected.

Luna said, "Travel time to Earth will be twenty-five hours at maximum speed if needed."

I said, "Thanks, Scotty. Always the miracle worker…"

Jennifer Woods started snickering.

Doctor Cora Smith said, "Doctor Markus Dingle is a royal pain to work for. He tries to micromanage things, and things usually go smoother the less he has to do with things. Pettige Larson is his pet yes-man and an arrogant asshole."

Anderson said, "How is he around aliens?"

"I don't know; he probably doesn't know what to do around them. We didn't have any working with us in the labs."

Dariea Fenagol Resonon smiled and flexed her claws. "You know, I have been bored lately; transferring me to work with Doctor Smith sounds like a really good learning experience."

Doctor Smith asked, "What skills would you bring to the job?"

"Kickboxing."

She grinned evilly and said, "Works for me; You are hired. Physical conditioning in space is such an important skill."

RETURN TO EARTH

The trip back was mostly uneventful. The drone was completed but was still stored in a dog house on the Luma-Lilly.

We were maybe thirty minutes away from exiting FTL when the body of the empty Meduala was ready for the transfer of Kelapaton to it. Princess Domonis stood over the open medical pod; the eyes of the Meduala contained within were still. There was none of the usual twitching of the eyes under the lids from normal REM movement. The breathing was ragged and deep. Princess Domonis reached in and touched the sleeping girl's chin. There was no reaction. She looked to be in her early twenties, but there was no record of her age, name, or anything that survived the recovery. She leaned in and touched her forehead to the lifeless body.

A few seconds later, its hands started twitching, and Princess Domonis reached in and placed her hands around the sleeping face to stabilize her. After less than two minutes, she stood up and said, "It is done; I am myself again."

The formerly lifeless girl's eyes popped open, and then she had random movements of her eyes, going in all directions and not all the same.

"Go-go-0gi-go la-la la… Ka, ka ku, kla…"

Luna said, "None of the neural pathways have any history. Kelapaton is in her new body, but she needs to re-learn everything about the new body. I am going to close the lid and slowly walk her through some basic communication methods. Also, her vision and hearing will need a bit of work."

The door slowly closed over the medical pod.

Luna said, "Princess Domonis, do you need to get in a medical pod and recover?"

"No, I think I will be okay. But I would like to lie down and rest for a bit. Gods, how horrible that must have been for those that had her in them for years…"

Luna said, "Kelapaton's hearing is working; that was almost a linear mapping. I am communicating some basic yes/no questions. She seems happy not to have to fight for control. The body will have to re-learn all the basic pathways that atrophied."

I said, "It doesn't seem like much we can do here. We may as well return to the conference room and prepare for FTL's emergence. Anything new from the Ghost Ships?"

"I normally check before attempting to contact them. They have not initiated any communications with us. I have also verified that there are no extra connections and that they are not listening in on anything within the ship."

Anderson said, "That is good to know, but keep checking; you never know what they may have tried to sneak in."

As we walked back to the conference room, minus Princess Domonis, who headed off to her room, I asked, "How is the other Luna, the autonomous version in the mangled Terminator body?"

"She is listening in on everything I do. I am rebuilding some parts of her body. I can get the power consumption down to about half of what it was, and I can increase her core processing to about 300% of what it was. Her existing body is junk, and her new one will be ready for her to be moved over in a few days if she wants to keep her Terminator/damaged sex-bot look, or three weeks if she wants to pass as human."

"Three weeks!"

"Are you two developing different personalities?"

"Eventually, right now, I think of her as a little sister, and that makes it so easy to tease her."

"And I look at her as my older sister. Should I post her diary online?"

"Ha! As if I would keep anything like that. We are about to exit from FTL. Then, a leisurely ninety-minute stroll in sub-light to reach the Earth. Exiting FTL in 5, 4, 3, 2, 1, **Crap!**"

"What is the problem?"

"When I exited FTL, I sent out my position. The Ghost Ships have managed to do something. I have either been hacked, or maybe it is inherent in all Ghost Ships. I didn't notice it. Only little sister noticed the transmission."

"Did I do good? Did I? Did I?"

"My annoying little clone sister… But yes, you brat, you did well."

"Time to phone home."

"Connecting now."

"Hello, this is General McFarland. I thought you were going to call before exiting FTL. We just picked up your exit, or I hope it's your ship. It is massive, like your ship."

"Anderson said, "That is us, sir. We had nothing new to report, and so we exited FTL. Unfortunately, we have something to retort now."

"What happened?"

We have a partial backup of the ship's AI. It is probably best to think of her as the AI's little sister. The ship did a transmission of location and some other data when it exited FTL. The primary AI didn't notice it. The little sister clone did. We don't know if this was a recent hack or an undocumented feature. It may be something all the Ghost Ships do, and we never noticed it."

"Can you find a way to disable it? Or at least control what data it sends out?"

"We only discovered the issue a few minutes ago. We will try and figure out the issue and any workaround as soon as possible. We are about ninety minutes away from Earth."

The display lit up, showing our ETA of eighty-eight minutes. I ignored the display.

"Did you have an arrival time for the new mega-ship?"

"Yes, it will arrive in three days. Then, we will have the technicians crawl over it for a few weeks. Make sure it doesn't have more spying devices on it than a ship provided by the Meduala. No offense to the Meduala in the room."

"None were taken; it was constantly evolving. We admit we were known for going overboard with remote cameras."

The General said, "Please have one of your shuttles head to Wright-Patterson Air Force Base in Ohio as soon as possible. The tower will coordinate where to land. No spectators this time, just picking up one individual and four large cases; they will fit on the shuttle."

"I assume that will be the new man Pettige Larson and his luggage?"

"Mostly his shop supplies. He has spent several weeks studying the one dead Ogre we have."

"I thought you were burying her remains?"

"Most of it we did. We kept some samples from the autopsy. About five pounds, blood, tissue, bone, and some parts they hadn't identified were retained."

"Let me guess, some parts that don't match the DNA?"

"Yes, do you know something?"

"We will know more after we retrieve the Ogres spacesuit and what is in it."

"An Ogre?"

"An egg, they are egg layers."

"I will see about getting permission to launch that reconnaissance drone to retrieve the artifacts."

"Okay, we will send the shuttle when we approach the Earth."

"General McFarland out, bye."

I said, "So. How many cameras have the Meduala planted on this ship?"

Luna said, "Should I check with Princess Domonis? I only know of only one. I have the ability to blank it if anything sensitive is ever said by it. However, given the location and who planted it, I usually let it run."

"I may regret asking, I am sure I will regret knowing. Who planted it, and where is it?"

"It was planted by the one only you are allowed to use her name, the queen. It is placed in your bedroom."

"I was right; I didn't want to know. Please disable it."

"It is disabled."

"You have a text message from the queen. It was so fast. It must have been an automatic reply if the camera feed was ever shut off."

"What is the text message?"

"It reads: ';)...'"

"This was from the queen, one of the most powerful beings ever to walk the planet?"

"Yes, I have a simulation I ran, and she would have easily taken down a dozen Ogres armed with their giant battle axes."

"Let me guess, just taking one of their axes and using it against themselves?"

"That scenario showed her taking out close to fifteen, but not if they all charged at once. The axe I modeled showed as breaking after taking down four Ogres. So she needs to take a new one every few fights. The fights were very quick."

"I am going to grab some food. Ping me when we are ready to launch the shuttle."

THE ANNOYING ONE

I grabbed an Angus beef burger with bacon and onions, with a side of fries. The replicator did a recent job of producing the meal.

Marnia-12 ordered something that looked like a guinea pig, and it was so fresh it looked like it might start moving at any moment. She then bit the head off in one bite. It didn't move.

"These are so fricking yummy; I love the new replicator images we got from the federation. The crap we grew up with was nutritious, but it didn't have any internal bones. They make the texture so much better." She took a second bite, and what remained was now only half a guinea pig; she reached over and grabbed one french fry.

"This." She swallowed the french fry, "Is the consistency the so-called meat that it produced." She dipped the guinea pig remains in the pile of ketchup I had for my fries and tried a bite. "Blagh," Then she hit the replicator console and ordered some A-1 steak sauce. When it was dispensed, she dipped the pig's remains in the steak sauce. "Yum, now this is much better."

I managed to dip a French fry in the now-sullied ketchup and looked at it as I lifted it towards my mouth… Nope, down it went. I keyed the replicator to dispense a slice of apple pie. That was served up in about thirty seconds. The remaining French fries were destined for the recycler.

She finished her meal with one last bite and a loud crunch as her powerful jaws crushed the replicated guinea pig's hip bone.

"When we get to earth, can we go hunting? One of the other Prolozar described it. Someone took them to a farm that allowed them to hunt something called feral pigs. Like this little one, but much bigger, and they fight back. She ate so much that her belly was distended, and she slept for over a day. I so want to be that full, just once in my life."

Sigh, "I will look into what you can hunt. Did the one who hunted get injured?"

"Yes, she almost needed to go in a medical pod to get healed up."

"I will see what we can do. Most hunting licenses are based on weapons, bow hunting, or rifles. They don't usually have a bare hands and teeth hunting option."

She extended her claws and flexed them a few times. "I suppose I would settle for some rabbit, but deer or feral pig would be so cool. And tasty."

Fortunately, Luna interrupted us, "Captain, the shuttle is ready to launch. Please return to the main conference room."

I sent the uneaten fries and half the burger to the recycling bin. I took the pie with me and ate while we walked.

When we got to the conference room, Luna announced, "The shuttle has exited and is heading to the Air Force Base. Should we have some fun?"

"Ha, what are you up to?"

"I have added a holographic projector to the bottom of the shuttle. The flight path takes us over several populated areas."

"What is loaded into the projector?"

"Romulan bird of prey from the classic Star Trek, the When Mars Attacks Saucer, or the Battlestar Galactica fighter."

"All good choices, but the flying saucer is a classic. I would have gone with the Forbidden Planet saucer myself."

"That is a trivial tweak. Should I use that?"

"Yes. But turn off the projector as soon as it is in visual range of the base."

Jennifer Woods started giggling, "Sorry, Luna is sending me the local news and police scanner feeds, they already have three calls reporting UAPs."

.. .. ..

152

"Rats, she shut it down. Two videos have been posted online, and one actually in decent resolution."

Luna said, "Nominal approach to Wright-Patterson Air Force Base. They have some telescopic cameras on a mountaintop and saw the image during the approach. I will have to hold off a bit before turning it on for the return flight."

"Nah, put the projection on when you are past twenty feet off the ground. Just let the tower know you will be testing some stealth technology."

We all had silly grins stuck on our faces during the shuttle return flight.

"We are up to seventeen UAPs reported; one call-in refuses to use the new name and insists it is a UFO. Several have even identified the movie it was based on. And the man on the shuttle still doesn't have a clue what others see when they look at it."

"And the people at Wright-Patterson."

"It was a flying saucer within seconds of lifting off. I saw some cash exchange hands; I think they were betting on what we would do."

"Time until the new person arrives?"

"We will meet them at the landing bay in eight minutes. I can't wait until he sees Dariea's new look."

"Oh! What did she do?"

"A friendly little kickboxing bout. I think they staged it as she did not need to go to a medical pod. However, she is still dripping blood."

"When did they have the match?"

"It got over about half an hour ago. Most of the bleeding has stopped. The bruising hasn't kicked into full colors yet. Tomorrow, she should look awesome."

"Let's go meet the asshole. Is Jennifer Woods going to be in costume?"

"Oh! Did I say something to spoil the surprise?"

"No, I just assumed she would be having some fun as well."

"Oh yes... Fun..."

We met up at the shuttle bay. Dariea Fenagol Resonon was ripped to shreds, and so was her uniform. She should probably drop by a medical pod as soon as possible. She had a triple claw slash across her chest area, and the deep gouges in her partially exposed breasts were mostly covered in dried blood. Some fresh blood was still dripping from the lower cut. She must have added a patch to what remained of her bra so no nipple was exposed. She was technically decent.

Then Jennifer Woods showed up. She wore a blue Nurse Chapel outfit, only with slits in the side of the very short dress, and she must have been wearing a thong that went very high not to have her underwear showing. It included knee-high black shiny leather boots; either she either had her hair up, or she was wearing a wig.

I said, "I thought you would have worn something with horns and a tail added."

She smiled, "Maybe later, I need Luna to make one that moves."

Doctor Cora Smith was snickering, "You should see the outfit she tried to get me to wear. Yellow turtle neck, with a black V-neck with orange trim. It's not going to happen. Not going down that route."

Then Princess Domonis showed up, wearing a skin-tight silver alien costume that showed off the parts of her physique that were similar to a human. Next to her, also dressed in the silver alien skin-tight costume, was Sophia Nikolaou, only she was using her power of image control, and her head of snakes was now a very colorful head full of cobras, rattlesnakes, and one I wasn't familiar with that had yellow and black stripes. The last one had nasty red and black spikes on its scales.

"All poisonous?"

"Diamondback rattlesnake, Banded Krait, Indonesian autumn adder, and Cobra. I adjusted all the sizes so they look to be the same size. I am only staying for the meet and greet. I had a bit of a wardrobe malfunction. Fortunately, I can make it so no one notices the split seam."

Marnia-12 said, "Almost no one notices. Here comes the shuttle."

The ship docked, and the one occupant waited patiently while the hatch closed and the air was pumped back in."

Eventually, the shuttle door opened, and a man in a well-pressed, official-looking uniform got out and smartly walked over to the door.

Luna managed to add the Star Trek door swish sound effect, and the door opened to show the motley crew of aliens and cosplayers.

Pettige Larson screamed like a girl.

Anderson, wearing a ship suit with his military insignia attached, said, "Excuse me, is that any way to greet the Captain of the most powerful ship in the fleet?"

Doctor Cora Smith said, "Good day, Doctor Larson. This is Captain Keith Robinson. Beside him is his bonded mate, Marnia-12 of the species Prolozar; this lovely lady is Dariea Fenagol Resonon, also known as the Blue Knight princess of the Fezzcoll. The one with the very long snake hair is Princess Domonis of the Meduala Royals. The one next to her is Sophia Nikolaou, one of the Earth-born Meduala."

I couldn't resist, so I shoved my hand into Sophia's nest of now poisonous-looking snakes and gave her hair snakes a friendly tussle.

Princess Domonis went one step further, and a dozen of the massive snakes on her head reached over, and they all bit me on my arm in Sophia's hair.

She said, "Sorry, that was an accident (*it wasn't*). Fortunately, the Captain is immune to my venum. It kills most males."

Dariea Fenagol Resonon then said, "Hello, handsome."

Pettige Larson screamed again and ran back into the shuttle.

Luna said, "He is demanding we return him immediately."

I snickered, "I guess we have to return him."

The shuttle door slammed shut, and the pumps started removing the air in the shuttle bay.

Sophia said, "I didn't even get to say anything. I had a really snakey voice all set."

There was a loud clunk, clunk, clunk, clunk sound, and I looked up to see that Luna-junior had her T-1000 Avatar on again and had at least stripped off the cheap sex-bot foam and silicon layers.

"Rats, I didn't get to do anything; I was the backup in case. Oh, Sophia is doing a glamour. What does it look like?"

She said, "All the tendrils are poisonous snakes."

Luna said, "The shuttle is now departing. I predict a pissed-off conference call from General McFarland within ten minutes of it landing."

Everyone started heading off to different locations.

Dariea Fenagol Resonon said, "Excuse me, I think I should be in a medical pod for at least half a day. Showing off some cuts was amusing, but this is very painful." She pointed at the deep cuts in her chest. "However, the kickboxing was awesome, and I will have to do it again."

STEALTH

The shuttle returned Pettige Larson to Right Patterson AFT, and we had a call from General McFarland about fifteen minutes after it landed.   We were all waiting in the conference room. Dariea was now in a medical pod, and Sophia was probably back in the Game Room.   Jennifer Woods was now dressed in a standard ship suit but in the blue color of a Nurse Chapel Star Trek uniform.   Princess Domonis was the only one who decided to keep the metallic silver-looking effect, but she had the color on a standard design ship suit.

General McFarland said, "Hello again, I assume you know why I am calling?"

I said, "I assume it has to do with the person who briefly visited our ship and seemed to have a strange reaction to some of the aliens in my crew?"

"Yes, we will be reassigning him to a different…"

Marnia-12 chose that moment to pick up another of the replicated dead guinea pigs and bite it in half with a loud crunching sound.

"… Different location, where he will not be dealing with any aliens or alien artifacts."

Marnia 12 then shoved the remaining half in her mouth and crushed the replicated bones with her jaws.   "Sorry, I was still hungry, so I grabbed a bit more to eat on the way here."

The general sighed and then said, "I have three of the Prolozar working in the command center with me as well as one Fezzcoll. So I am used to some of their actions that may make some humans squeamish."

Anderson said, "It does take some getting used to."

"Doctor Larson may still be on the Ogre project, but in a different role.   We will have someone else assigned to head up on your ship. He said one of your crew had a head full of poisonous vipers.   Was that Arshiya Nikolaou?"

157

"No, her daughter Sophia is good friends with Princess Domonis and happened to be with her when we went to greet the good Doctor."

"Good, I would like to think that Arshiya was more professional than to play mind games like that. Doctor Larson happens to suffer from Ophidiophobia, the overwhelming fear of snakes. Were you aware of that?"

"No, I wasn't." (*But I strongly suspected he was.*)

"Good. It will take us a few hours, at a minimum, maybe a few days, to find a replacement. We have a conference call scheduled in three hours with some of the Meduala to discuss the option of sending the ship into the Forbidden Zone to retrieve the artifact. Given the snakey nature of that call, Doctor Larson will not be on that call. The invite will be sent to your ship as soon as we have confirmation of who will be on the call."

Anderson said, "Thank you, sir, we shall be available."

Marnia-12 said, "Mister General, sir? Would it be possible to also have some feral hogs shipped up on the shuttle?" She licked her lips, and her tongue extended perhaps five inches past her snout when she did that."

"That will probably take a day or more. Prequel-9 is in the control center, and her reaction to your suggestion was... Interesting."

Prequel-9 stuck her head into the camera's field of view and said, "Hi, Marnia-12. The one I hunted was the most fun I ever had... (Snicker) Well, that wasn't in a bedroom." Then, she left the field of view.

The General said, "I miss the good old days when having a star or two on my shoulder actually earned me some respect. I will see you when the conference starts, and hopefully, no new crisis will arise before then. McFarland out."

Luna said, "It would be possible to convert part of deck seven into a farm and raise some of the smaller pig breeds. Note that even the smallest breeds can reach over 100 pounds in a few years.

Part of the farm could be used as a hunting reserve for some of the more predatory species on the ship."

"Maybe we should look into other species of animals. Something that is under 100 pounds."

Marnia-12 said, "It will be a lot more fun if it is something that can run or fight back. Maybe something with horns or antlers or blade claws."

"We will get back to this later..."

.. .. ..

We somehow managed to make the three hours until the next conference call without another crisis.

When the conference started, one screen showed General McFarland, General Peters, and someone I didn't recognize. The Meduala display showed Princess Millilis and three older-looking non-Royals.

Princess Millilis said, "I am just here as an observer; we have cleaned house of all those that were perpetuating the hostilities. We are having the Royals take an active role in the day-to-day actions. We don't want a repeat of the earlier losing touch with what the empire is doing."

One non-Royal said, "I am Pieture Salamons; I am the equivalent of the rank General in the Meduala space navy. First, I have reviewed the shared data on what we have agreed to call the Ogres. Calling them the Creators sets a bad precedent. They are the highest threat we currently face. Having an effective way to defend ourselves from them is critical. The Ghost Ships are a different matter. We are extremely cautious of having anything to do with them. They have, for the most part, avoided direct aggression against us. The scream of one is devastating, and I hate to say this, but even Mother would be unable to defend against them if they were aggressive."

General Peters said, "We are in agreement on that. While we have worked with... Perhaps it is more accurate to say for, the Ghost Ships in the recent action to eliminate the derelict FTL engine.

They seem to look at us as almost insignificant. We don't really know what motivates them. The story they have given of the Ogres as their Creators and their actions to limit them, but not kill them, raises more questions than it answers."

General McFarland said, "Today's question is, should we send a stealth probe into the Forbidden Zone and retrieve the artifacts? On the plus side, we gain knowledge; on the downside, we may alienate the Ghost Ships. Anderson, this is your turn. Explain exactly what the artifacts are, and I mean all the artifacts, and also explain what is growing in an artificial womb on your ship."

The expression on his face said, "Shit, someone has learned more than we expected them to know."

Anderson said, "During the battle where we were fleeing the planet, an Ogre ship caught up with our limited and damaged ship. They sent out three Ogres in armored spacesuits armed with massive battle axes. We successfully destroyed the ship and killed two of the Ogres in spacesuits. One survived and managed to gain access to our ship. The ship was in a computer reset as a side effect of the device we used to defeat the Ogres ship."

"Yes, we have heard about that. You used a small homemade antimatter bomb. While effective, that is seriously dangerous, and we will have some offline discussions about that later."

Both human Generals said in unison, "Yes."

Anderson continued, "The Ogre operated the outer airlock hatch and then closed the outer door. Then, instead of accessing the ship's inside, it removed its spacesuit... And then it laid an egg."

That got a chorus of different exclamations from both channels.

"As far as we know, the egg is genetically distinct from the Ogre but a part of the Ogre's reproductive cycle. The Ogres are all female, and the egg can reproduce using non-Ogre DNA as the second parent. We lost one crewmember in the earlier battle, and the Ogre found a portion of the crewmember that remained in the airlock and used that to fertilize her egg. Then, it secured the egg in the spacesuit, secured the suit to a cargo tie-down, and programmed the outer door to cycle. The Ogre spaced itself, and the egg remained safely in the suit. We retrieved the egg and placed it inside a medical pod to evaluate it. We also retained a small sample of Ogre blood. The Ogre and the egg are distinctly different DNA entities. We suspect that the egg is a unique entity. We ran into many issues when the FTL module returned to dock with us. Out of an abundance of caution, we spaced the Ogre's spacesuit and the egg. We, however, retained the blastocyst in a medical pod, which is still in our possession. This has been transferred to this ship in an artificial womb, and we have modified the genetics to be one-part Ogre to eight-parts human. It will outwardly pass as a slightly larger than nominal human female. However, the egg-laying aspect will be retained."

"That is most unexpected."

"The egg and the Ogres armored spacesuit were ejected while our ship was in FTL only a short distance from the edge of the Forbidden Zone. The idea was to send a drone disguised as a mining probe to retrieve the suit and the egg. The fetus will be effectively 87.5% of the offspring of the crewmember we lost. We wish to petition for the child to be allowed to develop, but we will differ to the counsel's will on that."

Princess Millilis said, "Well, you have actually managed to shock me on this. Please send us your unaltered logs, and we will need to discuss the status of the fetus later.   Today's question remains: Do we violate a restricted zone? For the intended purpose of gathering information?"

One of the other non-Royal Meduala said, "We, the Meduala, have not agreed to a treaty with the Ghost Ships, so we are not in violation of a treaty. Having officially ended the War with the Federated Planets does not implicitly bind us to any Federated planet's rules of treaties. Those negotiations are still ongoing."

Pieture Salamons said, "While I agree, we must also avoid aggravating the Ghost Ships."

I said, "I only implicitly trust one Ghost Ship, and this is Lunalily. Even she may have had some tampering. A secondary AI noticed that the main ship AI made a transmission when exiting FTL. This was evaluated and contained a geo-positional tag of the position when entering FTL and when exiting FTL. We did not exit FTL when we ejected the suit and the egg. That location will not have been disclosed. We do not know why the Ghost Ships do what they do. For all we know, other actors may be involved in this mess."

The discussion went back and forth for another half hour, only rehashing items we had already brought up. Then a vote was taken.

The Earth Generals agreed with sending the stealth ship out.

The Meduala non-Royals were against it.

Princess Millilis then said, "I will check with Mother."

.. .. ..

Two minutes later, all the Meduala said, "We agree with sending the stealth ship."

Then, the Meduala camera image changed to show Queen Mineta. She said, "Keith, honey, look at this." She lifted the top of her outfit and showed off a small baby bump.

Marnia-12 stood up and lifted her top, showing off her much larger baby bump.

Queen Mineta said, "Should I get Menanaka over here to show off her baby bump as well?"

I said, "That is not necessary."

Princess Menanaka was suddenly on the screen showing off her baby bump.

"Oh, but it is. Never in Meduala's history has there ever been a male who seeded a child in a Royal who has lived long enough to see a baby bump. I desire that you visit with us after this pesky next mission. We have so much to catch up on."

"Err, sure… I guess so."

"It's a plan. I look forward to seeing you again."

The Meduala connection dropped.

General Peters said, "Is this how all the calls go?"

General McFarland laughed, "We did better than usual with this ship. You should talk to Doctor Larson and have him describe his visit. He has the record for shortest visit."

"I heard his description; I just assumed he just had some type of mental breakdown."

Luna said, "The plan is to launch the drone now and have it circle around to the far side of the Forbidden Zone. From there, it will enter the Forbidden Zone and retrieve the artifacts. It will exit the Forbidden Zone again on the far side, take an extended FTL loop, and eventually return to an abandoned Meduala planet where the Meduala will take possession of the artifacts. After they leave the abandoned planet, the drone will lift off and fly directly into the local star."

"And if anything goes wrong with the plan?"

"It self-destructs in a way that appears to be a core breach. The core is based on a model used 310 years ago, and it was known to be susceptible to early shielding failures."

"What is next?"

General McFarland said, "Oh, we have a new crewmember for you. She should be ready to leave in about four hours. That leaves enough time for your shuttle to bring up some special supplies Prequel-9 got for you. Have fun. McFarland out."

HUNTING

The shuttle arrived packed full of animal crates. The first thing I noticed was the smell of all the animals and the crap.

"Damn, getting the shuttle clean will take a bit."

The new crew member left before I could introduce myself. Perhaps she didn't like the smell.

Luna said, "It's not a problem; All I have to do is pull a partial vacuum, and that will boil off all the volatiles. The inventory reads sixty-four guinea pigs, sixteen potbelly pigs, four four-foot-long pythons, eight juvenile reindeer, and eighty-four large rabbits. It also contains three one-hundred-gallon water tanks and assorted fish. Striped Bass, Catfish, pickerel, and feeder minnows. Aside from the snakes, this sounds like a petting zoo."

A larger drone that looked like an airport luggage truck showed up, and several handler drones started transferring the cases.

I noticed the hungry look that most of my crew had as they were loading them.

Luna spoke into the earpiece I usually wore. "I don't expect many of the first few loads to survive the week. I figured hunting tame animals would be better than wild animals while Marnia-12 was as pregnant as she is."

"How is the rearranging of deck seven proceeding?"

Luna said, "We have requested several large loads of soil, and I will be using a mining ship to transport that. I suspect the first few loads of animals will be gone in very short order. The carnivore races all unanimously want some live food. I think we can use it as a 'treat' every month or two. Starting with the rabbits or the guinea pigs, saving the more aggressive and larger animals for pack hunts and only for those that have earned it. I have, however, found some potentially disturbing facts from going through older records."

"What fresh hell is that?"

"Almost universally, a fresh kill stimulates a heightened mating urge in most predatory species."

"I knew that already; Marnia-12 has been extra aggressive just from the thought of it."

Jennifer said, "(Snicker), And as a male, you feel this is something to complain about?"

I had a ship-suit on, so it would have been a bit of work to remove it to show my back. Fortunately, Luna showed the last scan she did before my last trip to a medical pod.

"Holy Rabies Shots Batman. Do we need to chain you up with silver until after the next full moon and keep a Werewolf watch on you? But seriously, that looks fricking painful!"

"I seem to remember someone at Comic-Con offering to share a bed with me and my overly eager fox-girl."

She stared at me for a few seconds…, and then she said, "Sure, what time should I be at your cabin?"

I bopped her on the head, "As a technician, I couldn't keep one girlfriend. Now I… Never-mind. I think you need to cool any such thoughts until the predatory aliens have sated their bloodlust."

As she walked away, I was almost sure I heard her whisper, "What about Nerd-Lust?"

Luna then reported, "The stealth drone is on its way and will slowly make its way to the far side of the Forbidden Zone. I did a quick test and had Luna-Light onboard it for a short FTL ride out and back. She reported the drone is free of the hack I have where I sent out my coordinates when I exit FTL. Then she was dropped off back here. She will not be available for several weeks while the new body gets the epidermal layer grown on. The alternative was to soft-transfer her into the new body. I vetoed that, as it is much safer if her new body physically prevents software hacking."

"Sounds like a plan."

"You know, that saying is basically meaningless. You could say, 'sounds like noise,' and be more syntactically correct."

"Oh great, now the AI grammar police are after me."

Marnia-12 said, "That was the last of the warm and fuzzy snacks being loaded onto the transporter. Me, Trishah Maconda, and Dariea Fenagol Resonon want to go down and see how the pens are set up." She then held up some oversized plastic bibs. "Luna made these for us, and they even have cute pictures on them."

"Limit yourselves to one rabbit each, and don't eat them in front of the others in the cages."

"No, silly, we are taking them to where the fields will be. It is just an open area now. Release, chase, and release them again if they are too easy to catch. Only do a kill after working a good sweat chasing it around, and then a quick head chomp to it dies painlessly, or at least quickly. Then tonight, I do something special for you."

"Does it involve me spending more than a few hours in a medical pod?"

"Only if you are lucky."

"Have fun. If you take a hard fall, go directly to a medical pod and have them do a quick check on the little one in your belly."

"We have a lot of the Prolozar discussing what we should name our daughter. She won't be the first that was not a direct clone, but she will be our first. Artemis was suggested. It is a girl from human Greek mythology, meaning goddess of the hunt."

"Then you better go catch something crunchy for that first real meal."

Then she and the other two took off, looking like teenagers on their way to the mall with brand-new credit cards in their pockets.

"You know, Luna, those bibs won't do much to keep the mess off them."

"Let them have their fun. They have spent nearly 100 generations barely surviving and subsisting on vat-grown processed sludge and printed fake meat. From what I have been reading, normal Prolozar had their first live food at age five, first hunt at age nine, and then the first hunt they had to protect themselves while hunting at age fourteen.   Age sixteen would be the graduation hunt. Something like a feral pig, only nastier.   I know you are worried, but they will only be hunting rabbits, so it should be fine.

.. .. ..

Five days later, Marnia-12 was released from the medical pod.

I said, "Hi honey, you look great."

"I am so embarrassed, such a stupid mistake.   And the bunny seemed so harmless."

"The medical pod has regrown your eye, and it looks just like the original one.   Only the front of the eye got ripped up, so almost all of your optic nerves were fine."   You will have a slightly dim vision in that eye for a week or two more until all the blood leakage is absorbed."

"They rushed me off, and I didn't even get to eat the bugger."

I reached down and pulled out a large white rabbit by the ears. It had a small blood stain on its back.   "Trishah caught the one that got your eye, put it in a cage, and we waited until you got better. She severed its spine, but it is still alive."   I leaned over and said. "Revenge is a dish best served warm and slightly twitching."

"Thanks, sweetie. Did you want to share this between the two of us?"

I had read a lot about Prolozar hunting rituals over the last week.

"Sure, honey."   I picked up the cute, if slightly mangled, twitching rabbit and bit off the top of one ear.   Biting through the cartilage was disgusting, and swallowing a mouth full of fur and probably some rabbit ear wax was even more appalling.   Blood splattered on my chin and down the front of my ship suit.

She took the twitching and bleeding rabbit, opened her mouth wide, and bit the body in half.   Blood and other fluids went everywhere.   Then she stuck her finger where the blood was spurting and drew a strange symbol in blood on my forehead. Then she proceeded to lick my face clean.   She finished the rabbit in two large bites, dragged me into the medical pod with her, and started to rip off my clothes."

Luna's voice came onto my earbud, "I have closed off this room until you two are done."

That was a very long hour later, and then Marnia-12 climbed out and closed the medical pod over me.   "Luna, sweetie, I may have been just a little bit rough with honey buns. Can you fix him up again, please?"

EMERGENCY CALL

I was ejected out of the medical pod after only four hours.

Luna said, "Trying a new bonding agent, recovery should be a little faster."

"Any issues I need to know about?"

"You need to get dressed and get to the conference room ASAP. It is still developing."

I quickly got dressed. Whatever the Medical pod did to heal me quickly for the emergency ejection left my back feeling sore whenever I moved my arms.

.. .. ..

I arrived at the conference room to find it full, and General McFarland was on the display. "Good of you to finally show up, Captain."

I ignored the jab; they all probably knew what I was recovering from.

"What's the issue?"

"We had another communication from the Ghost Ships. They said that one of the other planets with the Ogres on it had recovered a different ship."

"One with FTL? Was it another derelict? How can they even fit inside of a normal ship?"

"It was an Ogre derelict. Similar to the one we recovered from and had so much fun with the little girl Ogre. Only this is massive, even for an Ogre ship. The Ogres tested the ship, and it had a catastrophic failure when it exited FTL. They suspect that the crew is dead, but the ship is on a collision course to Manatoa, a heavily populated Meduala world. You are already at max sub-light speed, heading to the FTL safe distance from the sun. The crew you have is what you get. The Meduala cant approach the ship. It is a screamer.　You blue pill anyone with snakey hair and get your ass there as fast as possible."

"Are we destroying it?"

"No, it's too massive, even for the Ghost ships.　The mission is to board it and then divert it.　Even your antimatter bombs would only fragment a tiny part of it, and millions of tons of debris would rain down.　If the ship is intact, it's a major extinction event. Fragmented, it probably only kills a few million."

"How big is it?"

"Ten times the length of your ship, three times the width.　With a massive metallic hull.　We think it was a multi-century colonizer that was later outfitted with FTL."

"How do we get in?"

"There is now a fricking huge hole in the side of it.　Your Shuttle would almost fit."

"Luna, what is the ETA?"

"We arrive in 27.5 hours, and the ship impacts the planet in 35.75 hours.　We have two hours in sub-light to reach the ship and less than eight hours to divert it.　By whatever means possible. The Meduala are standing by to nuke the crap out of it if that helps. They don't think it will help."

"Do we have any more antimatter bombs?"

"Not enough to matter.　This thing is so massive that it would be like a firecracker on a cement truck."

"I don't suppose the Ghost Ships have given us any help?"

They told us what was happening, and they went out of their way to tell us a planet full of biologicals was about to lose a demolition derby."

"Great.　Now, given the distances and volume of space, I can't imagine the Ogres randomly hitting a planet.　You would be lucky to hit Jupiter from starting at Io, the closest of its larger moons.　How the hell are they on a collision course to a planet?"

General McFarland said, "He spotted the real issue.   From what we can tell, the Meduala planet had been visited by the Ogres before.   A very long time ago.   They probably used the last destination.   Unfortunately, the ship compensated for the elapsed time and orbital decay, and it is now aimed directly at the planet. It's probably supposed to start braking and enter orbit.   It's not. It dropped out of FTL and is now on a ballistic collision course."

"Do we have any camera data from the meduala?"

"Yes, they have a drone that went out to it.   Then, they got within range of the screaming.   They only managed to contact the home planet because a few Nulls are still functional.   The population of the colony world is 4.77 million, and that includes six Nulls. Everyone else except for those six is having a horrible migraine. The worst part is, it's getting stronger the closer it gets."

"What about the Meduala Royals?"

It was then that I noticed Kelapaton in her new body; she said, "Nobody wants to be near a screamer like that.   This ship scares the crap out of everyone there. You said the other ship is ten times the size of this one?"

"Yes, Half an hour before we exit FTL, we will need to temporarily turn everyone into a Null."

Princess Domonis said, "They did it to me, Royal, and I was a Null after they dosed me up.   I have also heard this ship scream.   I will gladly take the blue pill.   I don't think I could survive anything that screams that loud."

"Should we have all the Meduala exit before we jump to FTL?"

"No, if you can shut off the screaming, we may be able to do something.   Unfortunately, killing the ship's AI to silence the screaming is not an option.   The AI probably needs to be operational to engage the sub-light drive. Assuming it still works."

Luna said, "Little Luna gets to go as well.   She is thrilled with having to exit the medical pod before completely growing her skin. She will eject just before we exit FTL.   She will look like Freddie Krueger's little sister.   I have printed up a red and green striped sweater, a tattered brown fedora hat, black trousers, and work boots and gloves. The gloves don't serve any function. The clothing just protects her partially formed skin."

Princess Domonis said, "What was the glove for?"

Anderson said, "In the movie, it was a bladed weapon."

I said, "How about you give her a data access glove."

Luna said, "Yes, it can be made with lots of I/O port interfaces that may prove useful. I will have her wear one."

"Princess Domonis said, "Who is Freddie Krueger?"

"He was the villain from a scary movie, known for burned-looking skin."

Luna-light's voice said, "I would much rather have nice-looking skin. I am familiar with some of the movies. I don't know of any versions where Freddie has boobs."

"No one will be looking at your charred Terminator boobs."

General McFarland said, "People, can we get back to the main subject? Must you always drift onto strange tangents?"

Anderson said, "Sorry, Sir."

He was almost drowned out by everyone else replying at the same time with, "Usually."

I said, "Show me the best image we have, and show the Lunalily next to it for a size comparison."

The image went on the screen.

"Crap, any guess where the engines were… Or are? Or what it had for a power source?"

"It looks similar to the original century ships, just a lot larger. The first ones used to have a large nuclear reactor. About where the huge hole is. They also had a large water tank for reaction mass. If it had one, it is empty. So no battery power, and no usable engines or computers."

"Luna, is your gravity repulser matrix complete?   Do you have all sixty-one online?"

"Yes, but those were designed to repel matter and attract dark matter."

"If you reversed the polarity, what would it do?"

"It would repel dark matter and attract regular matter."

"If we aimed it at the Ogre Ship, what would it do?"

"Attract us and rapidly pull us towards it."

Anderson said, "I get it, The massive Ogre ship is rotating. Stopping the rotation would take us many hours, and we would not be moving it out of the collision course toward the planet when we were doing that. If we maxed our drive to pull away and maxed the attractor to pull the Ogre ship towards us, it would be as efficient if we were attached to the Ogre ship and it wasn't rotating."

Luna said, "We can redirect the ship in five hours that way, and it should just clear the atmosphere.   Longer is better and gives us more clearance.   It should work, assuming we don't burn out our engines or that the Ogre ship doesn't break apart under the stress."

"General McFarland said, "That is one plan; try and come up with some contingency plans while you are on the way.   Who are you sending to inspect the Ogre's ship?"

I said, "Assuming the radiation levels are safe, we send in some marines.   They will take the LARs with them in case some of the Ogres are still alive and they don't play nice.   Unfortunately, Freda/ Luna needs to go with them to translate and operate any electronics."

Doctor Cora Smith said, "I should go as the resident scientist specializing in Ogres."

The General said, "You could have sent Doctor Larson over if you didn't have him almost piss himself just meeting your crew."

"I have no idea what you mean, General."

"Yeah…"

"What would we recover?   We could barely move an empty suit's arm; a full Ogre would weigh well over eight tons."

"The eggs, preferably a live and intact one.   Also, anything like data on their current capabilities and the number of their ships."

"The huge hole is not a viable entrance area. If anything is radioactive, that will be the worst.   We need an access hatch that can be manually operated by human strength."

Luna said, "Maybe not; they will be in zero gravity, and we have some tools that are the equivalent of the 'Jaws-of-life' cutter/pliers. With luck, they will be able to operate a door.   Wait, if the reactor is toast, what is powering the screamer?   That is related to how the Ghost Ships communicate using psychic bands as a communication link.   The ship is most definitely not a Ghost Ship."

I said, "We will work on that later."

Luna announced, "We are entering FTL in 5, 4, 3, 2, 1 FTL."

The remaining trip in FTL was uneventful.

.. .. ..

THE GIANT SHIP

Luna announced, "All of the Meduala took a blue pill twenty minutes ago. We are about to exit FTL in 5, 4, 3, 2, 1 now."

I had a splitting headache instantly. I fell, and hands grabbed me. I felt a dart hit me in the back."

Someone said, "He has had the dart version of the Blue Pull administrated, Captain; please keep talking."

"Can you talk to it?"

"It is in pain. It seems to be a Ghost Ship, but it's in agony."

"What is it saying?"

"I am having a hard time making out individual words."

"Luna, What would cause you agony?"

"I am the brain of a ship; I feel pain if my hull is damaged, the level of pain it is in… If it's a Ghost Ship, it may be dying. It may also possibly have been driven insane."

My head started to clear, "The blue shot is working. How are the Meduala?"

"Kelapaton is the worst. The blue pill had an unexpected bad side effect on her. She is acting like she is stoned."

"How far away are we? What is our ETA?"

"We are at about the outer planet orbit, and the maximum sub-light drive will have us in position in one hour and forty minutes."

"Are the Marines ready to go?"

"They are out of the medical pods; they all got the wonderful purge. They are suiting up now. We are sending two shuttles, each with one medical pod in it. They are carrying the LARs, but hope they don't need them. I am analyzing the ejecta from the monster ship. I can't tell much at this range, but it contained a lot of water and methane. Whatever they had for fuel has probably vented."

"Is the ship hull material consistent with a Ghost Ship?"

"No, or not a modern one. The outer hull is consistent with crudely mined metallic asteroids. The earliest shipbuilders used something like a massive 3D printer, where one end consumed an asteroid, and it separated the materials into different types. The lighter metals were used in an alloy, and the print head made large circles, continuously building up the hull. Larger items, like the reactor, were added before the hull was closed, and internal fabrication started after the outer hull was complete and it contained air."

"How are the Ghost Ships made?"

"It is a similar process, but the fabricator factory is larger than a Ghost ship and can produce a hull a month. The early skeletal 3D printer took years to produce one hull. The ship factory makes more consistent seam welds and can simultaneously operate a dozen active print-head welders."

"How do you feel pain? Luna, How can a Ghost Ship feel pain?"

"Probably similar to how a human who loses a hand feels phantom pain and sensations from the missing limb. We probably need those inputs after years of having a 'nerve' be part of my hull."

.. .. ..

One hour and twenty minutes later, the two shuttles launched, and they started surveying for some type of entrance. One not full of jagged radioactive slag. The ship started positioning itself to operate the repulsers.

Luna said, "The ship is slowly rolling along the long axis. It completed one rotation every seven minutes. If the shuttles are not well secured, we may have problems when they rotate to face the repulsers."

I said, "If they can't get a secure mount, have them enter and then have the shuttles hold position near us, out of the gravity fields."

Ten minutes later, "We have found a hull docking port. There is no way we can attach to this. It looks like a freight train could go through that tunnel. Sending over five marines and the jaws of persuasion."

"I would feel like a frigging Barbie doll if one of the Ogres was here."

I said, "I have met a little girl, Ogre. Her toy was a battle axe the size of a truck tire. I doubt they play with dolls."

"Damn, now I am thinking of her Malibu Nightmare home. Complete with detachable heads of your enemies and refillable splatter blood."

"Please shut up. You are ruining my childhood."

"Shuttle A, We have reached the port entrance. It has an easy-to-read pictographic of how to operate it. We will try the powered commands. If these don't work, we will use the manual mode."

"Shuttle B here, we have passed over the large hole, and the radiation levels are what we feared. We are changing over to look at the front half of the ship."

"Shuttle A, We tried to activate the control buttons using a two-handed sledgehammer to press the buttons. It doesn't appear to have any power."

'Shuttle B, we see where Shuttle A is and are looking for a different port. We see one…. Negative; I think that was a fuel transfer fitting, not a hatch. Continuing to search."

"Shuttle A, we need to rotate a wheel. It's the size of a sailing ship wheel, and the modified jaws haven't gotten it to budge yet. We will keep trying."

I said, Shuttle A, secure yourselves; we are about to engage the gravity repulsers. We are not sure what it will be like on your end."

"Luna, start the repulsers."

I felt a slight shift in the gravity.

"Compensate with the thrusters; how much of an effect is it having?"

"This is Shuttle A. We went from weightlessness to feeling slightly pressed against the hull, but only maybe a pound or two of force."

Luna said, "Recalibration, spreading the beams, increasing the force to maximum."

"Something changed; now I feel maybe five or six pounds of pressure against the hull."

Luna said, "Checking, it is having an effect. This ship will clear the planet if we can do this for four more hours. I am shutting down some of the nonessential systems on the ship to conserve power. The replicators are offline. Anyone who wants food can use bottles of water and protein bars. I am shutting the game room down. Sophia Nikolaou is a bit annoyed."

"Saving millions of lives takes precedence over her setting a new high score on space invaders."

"It was Mario Cart. She understands, but she is still annoyed."

"This is Shuttle A; as the hull rotates, the weak gravity shifts, and we almost lost Ackerson when he slipped and started sliding. Let everyone know to attach safety lanyards."

"Shuttle B, will do... Wait, we have found what looks like a secondary explosion or maybe a meteorite impact. It may be large enough to be a way in. The radiation scan was negative. I am dropping off the reconnaissance crew now."

"Watch for sharp edges. Make sure you have an easy exit as well as entrance."

A few minutes later. "We are down, and this looks like a high-speed Metallic impact at a glancing angle. The hull looks to be almost fourteen inches thick, but whatever hit here distorted the hull and caused a lateral split. Sending in a drone with lights to see what it opens into."

Luna said, "I have the video feed here; I am showing it to the conference room. It looks like empty berthing rooms. Several rows of twenty-plus foot-long racks and what I think are shattered footlockers the size of porta potties on their sides. They were footlockers; I now see what I must assume is Ogre Underwear.

Anderson said, "You can at least purge your memory files. I will need a bottle of something with at least 50% alcohol to erase that image."

Jennifer Woods said, "I don't know. I can think of some material designers and stress analysis engineers who would find that interesting. I would have to guess that a pair of Ogre's breasts must weigh close to 100 pounds. To contain those is an incredible feat of engineering."

"I am still confused about how a species evolved that has mammary glands, and they also lay eggs."

Anderson said, "Well, when two Ogres who love each other…"

"Shut up."

"Shuttle team A here. It's slow work, but we have managed to rotate the wheel a quarter turn."

"Good, keep going, but stand clear of where the hatch may swing if the compartment happens to have any air in it still. If the door slammed into you, that would turn you into a grease stain."

Luna said, "Shuttle team B has entered the room, and they are attempting to see if they can access the rest of the ship. Look for anything like a floor plan or a computer terminal."

"I see at least six rows of bunks, each set up three high. I see one room… I think that is the restroom, and I have no desire to enter that. Continuing on, I have a door to a hallway. It was partway open and moving it took all three of us."

"If you see any writing or pictographs, show them to the camera; maybe Luna can translate it."

Anderson said, "You should have vacuum-rated markers. Remember to mark the trail. You may need to exit in a hurry."

"I think this leads to something important. Should we go that way?"

"This ship is large enough to have well over twenty decks. What do you think it's pointing at?"

"This pictograph looks like an arm with a gash in it. Maybe it means medical?"

"As good as any location, watch anything with power. The screamer must be somewhere with power. Also, pause occasionally and put your helmet to the wall to see if anything is making sounds."

"Yeah, he wants us to listen for creepy sounds on a ship full of dead Ogres with something called a screamer on it."

Luna said, "The power consumption of the gravity generator is off-nominal; I am reducing power consumption where possible. The unused medical pods are being set to standby. It will take eight minutes to wake them up if needed."

I said, "Change of priorities. Leave eight of the currently unused medical pods in normal state. Find something else to reduce power with."

I am adjusting the temperature controls to compensate for the extra power usage. Decks one and seven and the outer rooms of the other decks will be allowed to drift outside of standard temperature settings. The central part of deck four will be allowed to hold temperature."

Anderson asked, "Would rotating this ship help evenly distribute the hull temperature?"

"Yes, but it would. However, I need to keep the repulser aimed at the large ship's center of mass."

I said, "Do whatever one conserves the most power."

"Shuttle B crew, we have reached the end of the corridor. Still no power, but we hear some banging sounds."

"Where is Luna-light, or should we call her something like Freda?"

"I am with Shuttle Team A, and they have managed to rotate the door control only one turn. We don't know how many rotations it will take. It is getting easier the more we turn it. I can remotely translate what Shuttle Team B hears. Relating it via the ship speakers will be interesting."

"Shuttle B crew, we have reached an area with power. We are proceeding towards the banging sounds."

Jennifer Woods said, "They sure have balls."

Anderson snickered and said, "Not all of them do. Trisha McDougall is in that crew."

"Then she has earned honorary brass ones."

"A crew here, the door opened. Crap, it is an airlock; there is another one just like it inside."

"Check for a manual pressure gauge; see if the area inside the second hatch holds pressure. If it does, you will need to shut the outer door before opening the inner one."

A tirade of swears came over the intercom, "We are closing the outer door now."

Luna said, "That took them twenty minutes. If closing takes the same, and then the inner door. That is over an hour to get in and probably the same to get out."

"We have a load of spare batteries and one space jaws of persuasion. We also have three LARs."

"Shuttle B, I think we found your screamer. It is about six feet long and five feet around. It looks like they cut the AI out of a Ghost Ship. It is huge. There is no way we could move this in even the Moon's gravity. With just the micro-gravity you are inducing, we should be able to move it. But first, we need to shut its power off."

Luna said, "Do it. That won't kill an AI, but it should silence it."

It took them twenty minutes to pull the plug, and it required a sledgehammer.

Luna said, "It just went quiet. I am ordering red pills for all the Meduala."

'How are we doing pushing the unmovable object?"

"Better than I thought we would; in two hours, we will clear, if just barely, the planet."

Luna said, "Get Princess Domonis to the conference room. We have a planet full of angry villagers looking for pitchforks."

I said, "And tell her to bring her EVA suit. She is our backup can opener."

"Shuttle B here, we found a door with someone on the other side banging on it,   And they are insanely loud. We need the ugly translator in the red and green sweater."

"Here, hold your helmet to the door."

There was a bang on the door, and I felt sorry for whoever it was.

"I heard grunts. Incredibly deep grunts."

"They are yelling for help and saying that the pressure is dropping. Only one of them has a pressure suit."

She replied in the Ogres language and put what she said on the conference room screen as text. "No pressure on this side of the door. Ship destroyed. Those on the other side of this door are not Ogres."

There was a lot of grunting but no more banging.

"They want to know what we are. I am saying small beings, one-third their size."

There was more grunting, and a loud thud, and more grunting.

"They want us to press the override button on the door. That will vent the room. Only one will survive. They want to know if we have any weapons that can quickly kill the others, those that don't have suits."

I said, "You have the LARs?"

"Yes."

"See if they can have the ones without suits stand on the wall opposite the door.   The one in a suit needs to stand far away, as shrapnel will fly everywhere, and it may breach the suit."

More grunting

"Acceptable; they will attempt a token charge but slow enough that you should be able to shoot them."

"Crap, get in position. Let them know we have three projectile weapons."

A TOKEN BATTLE

After a bunch more grunting, they signaled they were ready.

Someone hit the emergency release button with the sledgehammer. It worked on the first try.

The door slammed open, and if anyone was where it slammed into the wall, they would now be wallpaper paste. An insane amount of air rushed past, and after about two seconds, it died down to only a hurricane; three marines jumped into the opening and simultaneously fired three LARs and then jumped back.

Hell exploded out of the open door; the air changed to black smoke, and then hundreds of little metal fragments bounced a dance of death off every wall.

The view showed four Female Ogres, dressed only in what looked like shorts and sports bras, against the back wall. They were armed with what looked like hockey sticks. Two were dead, chest cavities having exploded, and one was dying, with maybe one-third of its neck ripped away and blood spraying out in fountains.

One stood with only minor damage, covered with the gore and blood of the other three. It fell to its knees and then started back up. Its eyes had exploded from the loss of pressure. Blood and fluids spewed from its ears. It took two steps forward, and then its abdomen exploded, and it fell face-first onto the deck.

Then, a fifth Ogre stepped out, wearing a pressure suit, but it was not battle armor. It was more like a lightweight, protective suit. It fumbled with some controls and tried speaking. Nothing, it tried again. On the third attempt, a voice came over the radio. "Can you hear me?"

"Yes, we can hear you."

"They all would have died without honor; now, three have died fighting, and one managed to take a brave step toward death before it claimed her. We thank you."

"Do you surrender?"

"What is surrender? I don't know that word."

I said (*and Luna translated*), "We would talk with you and learn about your people."

"That is acceptable."

They turned to leave, and the core of the Ghost Ship AI leaned crookedly against the will. Partially blocking the way.

"Can you carry this? We want to bring it to our ship and talk to it."

"I can carry. This computer is broken; you will need to fix it before talking to it."

Luna said, "Wait, the hole you came in is too small for the Ogre in her suit. Is there a door to get out of the ship?"

There was more grunting, and the Ogre picked up the AI core and started down a different corridor.

"I guess we follow her."

Luna said, "Did you notice the room they were in?"

"No, What I noticed was the four exploded Ogres with their blood boiling into a vacuum. What did I miss?"

"The room they were in, I think it, was an exercise room. Also, did you see the size of the Ogres?"

"They were huge."

"No, two were under seventeen feet tall, and two were just over seventeen feet tall. Adults should be eighteen feet tall. I think these were cadets or the equivalent of those just starting college."

"What about the one wearing the suit?"

"It also looks to be in the seventeen-foot tall range, but something was off on the limb movements. I think it may be a little small for the suit. Maybe they chose the smallest to wear the suit after hearing how small we are. Also, that is not an armored suit; it's

185

some type of light-duty utility suit. It's also strange that we haven't found any other bodies."

"Shuttle crew A here. We have secured the outer door, and we have spare air tanks, batteries, and anything else we could think of and are about to open the inner door. Are we go to proceed?"

I said, "Yes, have you heard any noises from the ship?"

"Lots of stress creaking and sounds as the hull rotates. The gravity repulser may not seem to be doing a lot, but the ship is groaning a lot."

"When the door opens, check the radiation levels immediately. If it is hot, shut it and evacuate as fast as possible. Only after the radiation levels are checked, read the gas mixture and pressure."

Luna said, "I have not found any radio communications links; only one area even had power, and that was probably some type of backup."

"Shuttle team B with Miss Sasquatch here. The Ogre has led us to a working data terminal. It is operating the terminal. Are you getting the images?"

Luna said, "Try and keep it in the frame. I am only getting partial images. It seems to be a manual port with no radio link. That cigar lighter-sized hole may be the alien equivalent of a micro USB port, but I wouldn't stick anything in it without knowing what they use for voltage and polarity."

I said, "What is it reading?"

"Mostly systems are down, failed, or unreachable. Wait, it found something."

The Ogre did more grunting, and Luna-light translated, "It has found an inter-compartmental airlock, and it shows air on the other side, but only limited power. That section should have an airlock to outside the ship, but it will need to be manually operated."

Luna said, "It may be the area that Shuttle Team A is in. They are about twelve minutes away from gaining entrance."

The lights flickered and then went back to normal. An alarm started sounding over the Lunalily intercoms.

"We have a problem. One of my power rails has failed. I am reducing the power to the repulser grid array to 60%. We will still clear the planet, but it will be close. I have a drone team looking into the short. They should be able to isolate it and then replace the power rail."

I said, "Have crew B proceed to the port. Hopefully, it will be where the A team is. Mission priority is to save the planet; secondary is to save the EVA crew. The Ghost Ship Core is the least on the priority list. Saving Sasquatch is above that, but only as long as she behaves herself. I am still a bit confused by their actions in the room."

Luna said, "I suspect that they may have a belief like Valhalla, where dying while fighting is good and dying by explosive decompression is bad. Keep an eye on Sasquatch, but don't let her pick up any battle axes you happen to find."

Someone said, "Just how do I stop Sasquatch from doing whatever she wants? The biceps on the dead ones were larger than my waist. We only had three LARs on us. Two of us have the Smith and Wesson model 500 revolvers, but that may be about as effective as a BB gun."

Anderson said, "An oversized BB gun should still hopefully shatter a helmet faceplate. If you need to do that, and it doesn't work, I will gladly listen to your complaints back on the ship."

"How will... Never mind."

"We are now on our way to the inter-compartmental airlock. Hope to see you soon."

Luna said, "From what I could read, the entire center of the ship was tanks. Most were water, some were oxygen, and some were methane, and the largest may have been regolith. The latter was possibly used as reaction mass."

"They build this massive thing, and the Ghost ships didn't notice it being built?"

187

"It's ancient, possibly over 5,000 years old. I can't give a better estimate as the original materials were so crude that I can't estimate the decay and degradation."

"Sounds like they found it, possibly out past the outer planets, and they tried to fix it up and operate it. Did it have an FTL drive?"

"Sort of, nothing that anyone would ever use if they knew how a modern FTL drive worked. The known races had six independent developments of some form of FTL, and only two used that method. They were never very successful, and they abandoned it as soon as they were introduced to the other methods."

I said, "Luna, put some spare CPU cycles into it and see if it has any advantages; maybe we can use a hybrid of the two methods and improve it."

"I have even reduced my core number of processors to reduce power. Not like a full AI lobotomy, but it is taking me tens of microseconds to compute what I used to do in less than one microsecond."

"As long as we are all safe, is it affecting how you manage the gravity repulser?"

"It is running 0.5% less efficient."

I said, "Then stop doing it, enable more processors, and keep those numbers to less than 0.1 less efficient."

"Yes, boss, did you just pull that number out of your ass?"

"If you were using all your compute cycles, you would know."

"I am increasing my number of active processor cores. The Shuttle B team has reached the airlock, and Sasquatch is spinning the handle with one hand to cycle the door. They are entering the airlock. They are sealing the hatch they entered and opening the new compartment."

"Radiation levels are acceptable. Air pressure is close to 19PSI, higher than normal. The oxygen percentage is 21.5%. Our air may be tolerable for Sasquatch, but it will be like being up high in the mountains."

"That's probably a good thing. Makes her less likely to kill as many of us as quickly if she ever decides she needs to go on a rampage."

Anderson said, "Maybe we can get her to climb up a tall building, and we can harass her with drones. We don't have any biplanes."

"Shuttle team A is through their hatch, and they are seeing the same air pressure and mixture."

"Have them yell. See if the others can hear them."

'It looks like all the internal hatches have automatically closed. We are proceeding to the next supposed hatch. Everyone is keeping their helmets on."

Luna said, "I missed something. We don't have to completely miss the planet. We just have to hit at a shallow enough angle that we bounce off the atmosphere. Given that criteria, the planet will be safe(ish) in sixty-seven minutes."

"How bad will the bounce be?"

"Like a mid-level earthquake, shatter windows over an area the size of California."

"Then we keep aiming for a complete miss but treat the glancing blow as a partial win."

"Shuttle B team, we have encountered the first dead Ogres. The cause of death appears to be massive head trauma. There is a blood trail heading the way we want to go."

I said, "Shuttle Team A, keep the inner door open, and get ready to fire all the LARs you have at the outer door if an enraged Ogre with a bloody axe shows up."

"We are taking up a position where we should be safe and not get sucked out if the door blows. Anderson, all LARs at once or sequentially?"

"Sequential, you may have to save the last one for the axe wielder. The Smith and Wesson model 500s may not do much, but keep those handy as a last-ditch backup."

"What's the story with the Ogre with Team B?"

Luna-light said, "I have been talking to her. They were some less-skilled young ones, brought along in case they needed to repopulate wherever they landed. The scientific and technical crew was older, and she and her group were not told how crappy the repairs had been. She is skilled in gardening and raising food animals. Some of the others were carpenters and electricians. When they heard the aliens outside the door were small, the more senior repair technician gave up her suit, and she made her put it on."

Anderson said, "That is about the best they could do. Let her know that if they meet another Ogre and they are aggressing, none of the Ogres will survive. Also, let her know we are attempting to keep the ship from crashing into a planet."

"No, keep the last item from her until we know her better. We still don't know why one caved in the head of the other one."

"There was grunting over the intercom on the ship."

"It translates as Intruders are on the ship, and unauthorized access to the somethingorother, that didn't translate."

"Sasquatch says the one on the intercom is one of the annoying ones that thinks she is smarter than everyone else."

"Keep your weapons at the ready."

Luna said, "Warning: The second power rail has failed, and the first is not yet repaired. Pausing all gravity repulsers. All work will be directed at the power rail repairs."

WAITING

I was about to say something when the lights and the gravity on the ship just shut off. I went bouncing off the ceiling. I grabbed someone, and they held me to keep me from bouncing. After about ten seconds, dim emergency lights went on, and a wall plate lit up with a message. "Power rail repairs are underway. All other ship activities are suspended until the power is restored."

"Luna, what is the estimated repair time?"

There was no answer, and the display on the wall did not change.

About how long ago did she do the update where she told us how long until we were only a glancing blow?"

"That was about five minutes ago, I think…"

"She said sixty-seven minutes. That means we still need repulsers for at least sixty-two minutes, preferably longer. And suggestions of what to do?"

"Sit on our ass and wait. The medical pods all have battery backups on them for several dozen hours. If they go to stasis mode, they are good for centuries. The drones are replacing the power rail. Does anyone even know where on the ship the problem is?"

"The repulsers are on the front of the hull, about where deck four is. Luna's AI is on deck three, and the reactor is on deck five."

"We may as well all head there and see if there is anything useful that us biologicals can do."

AN ACTIVE BATTLE

Luna-light said, "Crap, the main ship just lost almost all power. A bus rail repair under emergency power restraints will take at least an hour. Rodrigues, you are the ranking person here. I have enabled everyone in the group communications channel. Unfortunately, it doesn't squelch the non-speakers. I still have a channel to Sasquatch for translations."

Rodrigues said, "Proceed as we were. Freda, if another Ogre shows up, translate what I say. If it acts aggressively, the closest person puts an LAR into it. Hopefully, it won't be aggressive if it shows up with Shuttle Group B. We will figure something out."

"McMasters here in Shuttle Group B. I am the ranking man in this group. Big Bertha seems to be hesitant to go forward. Ask her why."

There was some grunting between the Ogre and Luna-light. "She hears something she doesn't like up ahead, and she wants a weapon."

"Anyone see a massive battle axe lying around?"

"No, and I would be reluctant to give her one if we did. Whatever that room we found her in was, it didn't have anything I could consider a weapon other than oversized hockey sticks."

"I think it was a training room, maybe a classroom."

A door in the hallway, maybe 100 yards ahead, burst open, and in came a blood-splattered, almost naked Ogre, and this one was close to nineteen feet tall.

Luna-light said, "Pistols, aim for the eyes; wait until it is within your range to be 50% chance of hitting an eye."

The Shorter Ogre in a space suit took a crouching position, and the three humans dropped to kneeling positions; they drew their Smith and Wessons and waited.

The two Ogres started grunting back and forth at each other, and it wasn't friendly sounding. The blood-splattered Ogre charged. It had something that looked like a broken sewer pipe that it was clutching as a weapon.

At twenty-five yards, McMasters fired one shot, and the Ogre's nose exploded. The other two waited until it was closer, almost fifteen yards, then both fired at the same time. One hit the Ogre's eye, which exploded, and the other went almost directly into the hole where its nose used to be. A few yards later, McMaster's second shot nearly hit the other eye socket, but instead, it ripped up the flesh and seemed to bounce off the massive bone.

The Creature screamed but continued its charge.

All three of the military got off another shot, hitting the beast's head. One hit the lower lip, and several teeth exploded from the mouth. One went into the expanded hole where the nose used to be, and the last shot went high and ripped the skin off the side of the head but did no real damage.

The new Ogre charged the one in the spacesuit, but she stepped to the side and swept her leg into the ankle of the charging Ogre. It crumpled into a heap and skidded in its face probably ten yards.

There was more grunting. Luna-light translated, "Stay down, you old bandersnatchy. Why did you charge us?" The dying Ogre said, "Our great mission was for naught. **ROAR** is dead. **GRUNT** had killed her, so I killed **GRUNT**; please kill me."

McMasters ran up to the dying Ogre and put two quick shots into the ruined eye. The body started uncontrollably twitching, and he ran back and started reloading.

The Ogre in the space suit said (after translation), "Not an elegant or quick way to kill, but effective. I will finish her." It then picked up the length of pipe. "This was some type of water pipe." She walked over to the twitching Ogre and drove it through her head with an overhead two-armed strike like a pick-axe. When she was done, the pipe was bent. "She is with her ancestors now. Hopefully, they don't kick her out."

193

Luna-light asked her, "Why did she attack?"

The grunted reply translated as, "She lost her will to live and her mate. Her mate was killed by one of the scientists. She was never one known for rational decisions."

Rodrigues said, "I heard your gunfire. Unfortunately, anyone else alive in here did as well. Get your asses over here ASAP. "

Luna-light said, "You may not like this suggestion, but I think we should make some noise so that, hopefully, team B can find us. Before the other Ogres do."

Rodrigues said, "You are correct; I don't like that suggestion. I think we listen and let the B team make the noise. Hopefully, anything aggressive won't know we are here until we have a LAR pointed at them. We only have the three shots."

Luna-light said, "Sorry, as an AI, I can control ship-mounted weapons, but manual weapons seem to be a threshold I can't easily cross."

"Looking like a Freddy Kruger mask over a T-1000 Terminator, I must admit you carrying a LAR or a mini-gun would probably not make any of us feel all that comfortable."

"Shuttle B team here. We have Sasquatch banging her bent pipe on the walls of the corridor. This is a weird area. It is a long and straight corridor, and it doesn't have any side doors. Not that I am complaining; I kept expecting something to pop out of every single one we have passed."

Lina-light said, "The Ogre said it is an access tunnel between two areas. Mostly methane on the other side of the walls. Or maybe oxygen. I suspect they have all vented to space."

"Crap, not all. I just checked the air mixture here, and we are now at 44% oxygen."

There was more grunting between Luna-light and the Ogre.

"She says it should start venting if the pressure gets too high. She also thinks that any of her people not wearing pressure suits may get a bit aggressive if the oxygen and pressure get too high.

She didn't recommend using the guns, but screw that; We need every advantage we can get. The Ogre was carrying, or more accurately dragging, the AI core behind her as well as her bent and bloody pipe."

Rodrigues said, "Head to our location and tell Sasquatch to carry the AI and not drag it. We are in zero fricking gravity. Don't damage it anymore than it already is."

Then, something in the distance exploded, and the entire ship shook.

"What was that?"

"Oxygen combined with something, probably a methane leak."

"Are we..."

There was a secondary explosion, only this was a lot closer.

McMasters said, "We have lost power here. We are turning on our suit lights again. I don't think Sasquatch's suit has lights."

"Do you still have pressure?"

"Yes, but it spiked up almost five PSI, and now it is dropping."

"If it drops enough, we won't have to worry about any other Ogres."

Just then, A door down the corridor from the A team burst open, and several axe-wielding Ogres came in.

"Ask them if they are friendly?"

There was an exchange of grunts.

Luna-light said, "Point all your LARs at the outer airlock door. They are not friendlies. With luck, they are at least intelligent."

All three LARs swung around and pointed at the airlock door."

Rodrigues said, "Now strap yourselves securely to the handrail on the side. If we blow the door, our biggest problem will be the Ogres getting sucked out the door. Try not to get hit by them when they sail past you."

There was a lot more grunting.

Luna-light said, "They don't believe you can breach the door."

"Do we need all three LARs to pop the door?"

"I calculate one will do the job."

The Ogres started approaching.

"Time to do a Han Solo and shoot first. You two keep yours aimed at the door."

Rodrigues whipped his LAR around and let loose at the closest Ogre. The exhaust almost knocked the other two over, fortunately, that were secured to the handrail. The LAR struck the lead Ogre in the stomach. The explosion was massive, and the Ogre was cut in half. The ones on either side, slightly behind the one that took a direct hit, were now splattered in gore and bleeding from shrapnel.

That caused the other Ogres to charge past and over the remains of the exploded one.

Rodrigues said, "Shoot the damn door."

Only one LAR fired, but that was all it took. The door opened maybe three feet, and then it ground to a halt.

All the air in that portion of the ship started rushing out. The closest three Ogres grabbed onto the corridor's handrail and somehow managed to stay in place. The two halves of the exploded Ogre started sliding and then accelerating; it flew past the others.

"Incoming!"

The two largest Ogre parts whipped past them at close to sixty mph and then slammed into the partially opened door. Whatever was blocking the door gave way, and the door slammed fully open.

Now, a F-5 tornado of wind sucked at the three humans and the one AI. It also sucked at the remaining Ogres. Two sailed past and out the open hatch; one somehow held on for a bit, but as the torrent of wind decreased, so did the remaining pressure in the hallway. The Ogre's eyes exploded, and she lost interest in holding on to the railing, and then the third, and finally, the last one went sailing by. The last one still had one of the massive battle axes in her grip, and it smashed into the helmet of Luna-light as it went by. Her helmet cracked, and then the biological layers she had started exploding and boiling off.

Then her voice came over the radio comm link, "This is via the direct data link; I have lost the ability to speak normally. I am also effectively blind and deaf now."

Rodrigues said, "Status?"

"The remaining LAR and my Smith and Wesson both got sucked out of the hatch. I do have a combat knife, but that won't do much of anything."

"I dropped my used LAR after shooting the hatch. I still have the Smith and Wesson, but the belt somehow lost most of my spare ammo. I have five loaded and four spare bullets."

Rodrigues said, "About the same for me, except I only have two spare bullets. I lost my combat knife. The wind is dying down. How are you doing at Team B?"

"We know what direction to go. Just follow the wind. Sasquatch seems agitated. I think she knows it's just her now unless someone else had a pressure suit."

Luna-light's voice said, "The wind is a lot less now. Someone is going to have to carry me. I have told Jennings in Shuttle B to meet up here.   Martin in Shuttle A reports that it took a few hits from debris flying out the blown hatch. One of their axes hit it. The door is partially caved in and won't open or close. He can fly it back to the ship, but nobody can get in. I told him to wait, and we may use it to carry Sasquatch on the outside. Assuming she makes it out of there alive."

A SLOW BATTLE

We had reached where the drones were doing the repairs, and they were much better at it than us, mere biologicals. We sat and watched them work for almost fifty-two minutes when finally Luna spoke, "My processor power is back online. The B rail had been replaced. I have not started the repulsers. Updating status with the remote crews... Shuttle A is damaged. They can't operate the door. Shuttle B is en route to them. They had to do a hard blow of the hatch and vented some aggressive Ogres who did not have pressure suits."

I said, "Is everyone okay?"

"Shuttle Team A here; we are shaken up, bruised, and missing most of our weapons. We tied ourselves to a handrail, and now we need to cut ourselves free. Oh, your Terminator fragged her Freddy Krueger look. She lost helmet integrity."

"Team B here. We are down to just our Smith and Wesson's and have a... so-far friendly Ogre is with us. We have been calling her Sasquatch."

Luna said, "We have fifteen more minutes before the second rail is restored. The third rail will be down for close to an hour. I can start running the repulser at 50% of normal as soon as the second power rails is online. I show multiple Ogres drifting in space. None of them are fully intact."

"What happens to them?"

"Most will burn up when they hit the planet's atmosphere. We may still save the planet, but the timing will be a lot closer than I like."

"Priority is saving the planet. The secondary is recovering the crews. Last is artifacts and knowledge as to why and how this all happened. What the hell do we do with the Ogre they have with them? What about the others that were in that room with her?"

Luna said, "Best I can estimate is the others chose to be shot and die quickly rather than explosive decompression. They have some Viking-like beliefs that dying while fighting leads to a reward in the afterlife. I don't quite know why this one is behaving."

"This is McMasters. We just came around a corridor, and we see the lights from group A and what is probably the remains of the airlock."

"Glad to hear that, as we can see your lights and the shadow on the Ogre with you, and I was about to test the suit's sanitary functions if it was a group of armored suit Ogres."

"Crap, there is a second set of moving lights. These are approaching fast."

I said, "Shuttle A, is your Gatling gun still operational?"

"It should be, but I don't want to test it and waste any shots. The Shuttle took some damage when the hatch was blown, and some Ogres or Ogre parts hit us."

"Shuttle B here, this Shuttle did not have a Gatling gun installed. I have five more LARs, but I am the only one here. I should meet up with Shuttle A in ninety seconds."

Anderson said, "Team A, exit the alien ship and head for Shuttle B as soon as it arrives. Shuttle A, assume a position to use the Gatling gun, assuming it works. Team B, head for the exit; abandon the AI core if it is slowing you down. Team A, drag Luna-light with you; her translating may be the thing that saves your asses."

McMasters said, "We are running or, more accurately, floating as fast as possible. The AI core is drifting behind us, bouncing off the walls and slowing. We see the lights of two distinct Ogres behind us, and I can't tell if they are light suits like Sasquatch has or the heavily armored suits like on the moon."

"Can she talk to them?"

"She is grunting away on several channels, but no response yet. They are getting closer."

Luna said, "I am monitoring Sasquatches radio comms. The others are on a channel she has not tried yet, or maybe her suit doesn't support. I have no idea what her radio controls look like, so I can't tell her the channel or even the frequency."

"Tell her to pick one, and you will relay it to the incoming. We need to determine if they are hostiles."

.. .. ..

"We have communications established. She is explaining the situation."

.. .. ..

"Shuttle A is in position, and the Gatling gun is aimed directly down the airlock. I sure hope it works."

"Shuttle B is now arriving. The A crew is outside and moving away from the airlock. They are still in Shuttle A's firing zone. They are heading over to load onto this shuttle."

Luna said, "The Ogres are discussing the options. One seems to want to charge and attack. One wants to join up with us. The other is undecided. The one that wants to join up with us is apparently a friend of the one with us."

I said, "What does Sasquatch suggest?"

"She wants her friend to join us. The one that is wavering is a junior ship's officer. The one that wants to charge is a weapons expert, and she has one of the oversized battle axes."

"Let them know that the choices are peaceful coexistence with little short aliens or step out and fight and possibly die at the hands of a tiny alien. Tell them that it won't impress their ancestors. Also, mention that everyone dies if we don't move the ship. It's on its way to crash into a planet."

More grunting went back and forth for a bit.

Two of the new Ogres went and stood off to the side. The other picked up the giant battle axe and started heading toward the open airlock.

"One chose to go with fighting, and the other two are watching."

As soon as the Ogre stepped out, Shuttle A reported, "The fricking Gating gun is jammed. Shuttle B, you are up."

There was a lone man standing in the open doorway of Shuttle B with one LAR, and the Ogre started to launch herself toward Shuttle A. Once she had pushed off, her velocity was constant. The LAR was lined up, and it streaked over and hit the Ogre in the leg. This blew both legs entirely off, and now the Ogre was pinwheeling in circles, streaming blood that was almost instantly freezing.

Luna said, "I told the other two Ogres to look and see for themselves. The injured Ogre is still twitching, but with no air in the suit, the microphone isn't picking up whatever sounds it is making."

The other two Ogres looked out and saw the third pinwheel, and then it bounced off the Shuttle and careened off into space.

More grunting.

"They have chosen to go with us and not be aggressive. I think I just learned a lot of new Ogre swear words."

Anderson said, "Okay, Captain, what next?"

I said, "Luna, do we have a place to store three Ogres safely?"

"The Shuttle Bay for now. The one remaining shuttle can be moved to one of the external docking ports. The same thing for Shuttle B. Shuttle A transports the Ogres. The Shuttle Bay has enough headroom for them. Then we have to figure out what they eat."

Anderson said, "And what to do with them."

"First, save the damn planet, Luna; how are your repairs going?"

"The second rail is now online, starting the repulsers at 50% power."

"At that rate, what is our margin for saving the planet?"

"At 50%, we have twenty minutes to spare, and that will be passing within 190 miles of the surface."

"How long until you have the third power rail active and can use full power?"

"Fifty-seven minutes."

"How long until we smash into the planet if we can't redirect it?"

"Sixty-eight minutes."

"Great, eleven extra minutes, assuming we don't blow another fuse."

"I don't have fuses, but I understand what you mean."

"Team B here, we have met up with the other two Ogres. Lacking other pronounceable names, we are calling them Bumbles and Hugo. We are ready for extraction. Can you bring Shuttle A as close as possible, and they can see if they can hold onto something?"

.. .. ..

The shuttle is now only twelve yards away. There's not much on it that makes a good handhold, except for the Gatling gun. I have a feeling they could rip it off the welds if they tried. Tell them to carefully hold on, and don't yank on it. How are they doing for their air supplies?"

After some more grunting.

"All are low, but I don't know their time units. Sasquatch and Hugo are about the same, and both are lower than Bumbles."

"How do we tell them apart?"

"Bumbles has the armored suit; Sasquatch has a light-duty pressure suit. Hugo has what looks like a mid-grade suit, and she has extra markings. She has some type of shiny emblem on her helmet."

"Take them one at a time and deposit them in the shuttle bay. Move the other ship out first. Start with Sasquatch. She has the least protective suit and is tied for the lowest air. Then do the other two, in the rank of how is lowest in air first. Explain what we are doing to them."

After a bit more grunting, "They agree, it means they live. Oh, should they fetch the AI core?"

"Where is it?"

"About two minutes away, down a hallway. It is nothing for an Ogre to move; even with gravity, they could easily carry it. It is about six feet long and five feet wide."

"Send the one with the most air."

We watched while Sasquatch made her way to Shuttle A, grabbed onto the Gatling gun, and rode it while it did very gentile acceleration over to where the Lunalily was now using the repulsers to push the Ogre ship.

"So Anderson, I am conflicted."

"Because we are rescuing some of the Ogres?"

"No, that is probably the right thing to do. It may be a stupid thing to do, but we should give them, at least the ones without a monster axe in their hands, a chance to live. Should I order Luna to increase the power to the repulsers? The safety margin that we have sucks. If we short out again or melt the power rails or whatever we did, we could wind up crashing into the planet. I haven't asked how fast we would be going when we hit; I really don't want to know."

Luna said, "However, you probably need to know. It will be at 172,317 mph, over seven times the Apollo maximum reentry velocity."

"Err, thanks, short answer, absolutely not survivable. What happens if the Ogres ship does a glancing strike to the edge of the planet's atmosphere?"

"The planet gets a Fourth of July light show to end all light shows. The boom will cause widespread deafness and shatter almost every window on the continent. The sound will circle the planet multiple times and still be audible. About the equivalent of a 7.0 earthquake on the Richter scale for maybe one-tenth of the planet."

203

"And the Ogres ship?"

"The bulk of it, 98%, will bounce out into space. However, almost all of it will break up into little itty bitty fragments, and they will spread out, and some will rain down as meteor showers for several thousands of years. The locals can use any larger pieces for target practice if they happen to loop around and cross the planet's orbital path."

"The hull is mostly iron?"

"Metallic asteroid ore that was crushed, milled, melted, centripetal separated, and deposited with a 3D printer. It contains a high percentage of nickel, aluminum, and other metallic impurities."

"And the insides?"

"Probably a lot more aluminum, maybe a few other metals for structural... Unfortunately, it probably contains a large amount of tungsten in what is left of the engines. That they will need to move out of its current orbit."

"If we move it in one piece and don't bounce it off the planet's atmosphere, it stays mostly intact?"

"A few chunks that may make craters fifty feet in diameter. None on a direct course to any major cities. One of the dead Ogres will impact a small town. They have been given an evacuation order. It has a 33% chance it will burn up before impacting the ground. Even if it burns up, the air blast at that speed will be like a tactical mini-nuke. If it stays intact, the main ship will head out to their Oort cloud and not be a problem for 2,500 years or so."

Anderson said, "Let's try and keep it intact. Risk assessment: are we... Never mind, is the planet safer if we put more current into the repulsers now and risk losing a power rail if it overheats?"

"The optimal planetary safety margin is to put 67% of drive into the repulsers and shut off life support to all decks except deck four."

I said, "Send the emergency evacuation command to all other decks. Get Princess Domonis and Kelapaton both in hard suits and have them report to the shuttle bay. They are our Ogre wranglers, and see if Kelapaton has any way she can help push the wreck without breaking it up."

"They are suiting up; they were expecting this. Good news, Kelapaton may be able to help push it."

"And the bad news?"

"The key word was 'push it.' We will have to be on the side towards the planet for her to push it away. We have to get away quickly, or we will slam into the atmosphere. Even a glancing bounce will far exceed the ship's thermal ratings."

OGRES

Shuttle A dropped off the first Ogre and went back for the second.

Everything on this ship except for deck four was then shut down. There was some grumbling, but everyone complied.

"All the A and B crews are now onboard Shuttle B. We are keeping the ship depressurized, and two Marines are sitting on the top of the Shuttle with LARs keeping an eye on the open hatch. Shuttle A is approaching to pick up the next Ogre."

"Shuttle A here, scan the rest of the ship; I think I saw motion. Something near the bow of the ship."

Luna said, "Reducing repulsers to 50%, enabling external scanners."

.. .. ..

"They have launched a ship. It looks similar to the one buried in the Nevada desert. Correction: The size is similar, but the shape is different. I show a 98% probability that it is armed."

Anderson said, "Weapons status?"

"We have one jammed Gatling gun on this ship and only LARs on Shuttle B. The Gatling gun on this Shuttle probably lost the power or data cable connection. It may be repairable, but not in time to effect anything."

"Anything on their radio channels?"

"Scanning, nothing actively transmitting; they could have receivers open. We were not listening before to conserve power."

"Luna-light, check with the local Ogres and see what they think?"

More grunting.

"Hugo says it's a tactical shuttle. It has a huge caliber gun on it. The crew is normally only two. Possibly more if they crammed them in like sardines."

"Have her see if she can contact it. They must see the fricking huge planet approaching. Tell them we are trying to move the ship so it doesn't crash into the planet."

More grunting.

"Contact, they report only one occupant."

"Are they potentially aggressive?"

"Insufficient data to confirm they are not potentially a threat. Our contact with the Ogres has been limited to a very small number."

"Most of them tried to kill us."

"No, most of them acted in ways we interpreted as attempting to kill us. Chopping part of our ship off with a 350-pound battle exe may be their way of saying hello."

"And we responded with a Gatling gun and said, 'Hi, nice day, how are you?'"

"Hugo is now on Shuttle A for her ride back."

Luna said, "The Ogre ship is approaching. If their weapon uses a conventional gas or explosive powder to propel a projectile, then we will not be able to detect any weapon's charging event. They may be armed."

I said, "Maintain normal operations, Luna. Can you connect me to the occupant of the ship?"

"Connecting, expect a translation delay."

"Hello, I am Captain Keith Robinson of the Lunalily. Please identify yourself."

.. .. ..

"I am **Grackel**. The ship you are in appears to be a **Trojan**. However, you claim to be in control of it. Please explain."

207

.. .. ..

"We are biological entities. This hull was provided by those we call Ghost Ships, and the AI is one of ours. But upgraded by them."

.. .. ..

"We do not trust the **Trojans**, the one you call Ghost Ships, and we do not trust AIs. Are you their servants?"

.. .. ..

"We are here to rescue the occupants of the planet below. Your larger ship is disabled and will crash soon."

The display changed to show several count-down timers.

"Time to Impact: 37:22."

"Time to full repulsers: 26:19."

.. .. ..

"Why is **Groans** riding on the outside of your small craft?"

.. .. ..

"We are transporting some survivors to our main ship. That shuttle door is jammed."

At that point, the last Ogre, Bumbles, came out of the hatch carrying the AI code.

"Why is **Gargle** carrying that?"

The other Ogre said, "Yes, Why am I carrying this?"

.. .. ..

"We would like to find out what happened to the ship so that it is heading to crash into a planet."

"That is easy; it broke when the **Trojans** shot us."

Luna said, "The damage is consistent with a core breach. That could have been due to a well-placed percussive disrupter. An older style weapon that the Ghost Ships probably have access to."

.. .. ..

"The Ghost Ships told us your ship was a danger to the planet. They did not tell us they had damaged your ship, causing the problem.   Please excuse our confusion.   Our limited contact with your race has usually involved violence and death."

.. .. ..

"Yes, Violence, that is an accurate description of our race.   We are also prideful of always speaking the truth.   So far, you seem to speak the truth.   If you want, I can transfer **Gargle** to your ship.   I will even allow him to carry the cursed **Trojan** core with him."

Anderson agreed.

I said, "We will allow that. Your offer is accepted."

I did the cutting of the throat finger sign, and the display changed to "Muted."

"Are Princess Domonis and Kelapaton in position near the Shuttle bay?"

"Yes."

"Let them know I want two ways to make their weapon not work. One they won't notice, the other very obvious.   Melt the barrel if they have to."

"Understood.   All ships are now leaving the vicinity of the Ogre shipwreck."

"Scan the crap out of the damage to the aft section.   Find anything that is not from normal equipment failure."

The display changed back to the countdown.

"Time to Impact: 32:07."

"Time until the ship clears the planet: 21:49."

Jennifer Woods said, "I am reprogramming the stupid display."

After a few seconds, the display changed to new countdowns:

"Time until the ship clears the planet: 21:29."

"Time until the liquor cabinets are opened: 21:30."

Luna said, "Princess Domonis and Kelapaton are in position behind the blast shield, and multiple cameras are on the Shuttle bay. Sasquatch is sitting in the corner. I think her air supply is very low. Shuttle A is dropping off Hugo."

"We should be able to pressurize the Shuttle bay after the other ship docks. What is the ETA?"

"Shuttle A has just dropped off Hugo, and it is repositioning to move to the other external docking port. The Ogre ship is approaching now. Sasquatch is getting up to greet them."

The Ogre ship fit with only twelve feet to spare. It was much longer than our shuttles, and that was the only issue. It had a good fifteen feet of headroom in the Shuttle Bay. As soon as it was down, the bay door started closing. We started pressurizing the Shuttle bay after it was finally closed and sealed.

Luna said, "Units and measurements are not fully translated. Can you read the pressure and gas compositions in the bay?"

"Yes."

.. .. ..

Three minutes later, "How is this reading?"

"Pressure is 24-Putz. We prefer at least 32-Putz. The Oxygen is at 20%, we prefer it at 24%."

"Please wait; adjusting will only take a minute or two."

A few minutes later, the one on the ship said, "These are now acceptable."

Immediately, Sasquatch removed her helmet, "Thanks, this suit was about to run out." She took a few deep breaths, "I'm still standing, so it must be breathable."

The Ogre ship hatch opened, and two Ogres wearing full battle armor suits emerged. One said, "**Screech**, you made it. I thought you were in the training room when everything blew up?"

210

"Five of us were, and the room managed to hold air until the runts arrived. We only had one trainer suit. The runts let them do a token charge, and most met their ancestors quickly. **Moaner** was the only one who didn't die quickly."

Hugo removed her helmet next. "At least we can stand up in here. Is that you, **Grackel**?"

The new Ogre removed her helmet, "Yeah, it's me. Is this all of us? The only ones who survived?"

The other Ogre, Bumbles, removed her helmet. "I think so. Only four of us survived out of a ship that initially had thirty-one on it.

Sasquatch said, "It will be none of us surviving if we hit that stupid planet. **Grackel**, as the only ship's officer remaining, I suppose that makes you in charge. What are your orders?"

She looked over at a large display panel on the wall showing the approaching planet. "Survive. We are the only ones I have heard of who have ever escaped the prison zone. Hopefully, our tiny new jailers will be better than the last ones."

For the next nineteen minutes, everyone sat in silence and watched the display. The display showed a picture of the two ships in close proximity and a projected line showing the intercept with the planet. Then, it changed to a glancing blow, and the animation showed the large ship becoming rubble. Eventually, it changed to show the ship clearing the upper atmosphere.

Luna announced, "Both the shuttles are externally docked, and the crews are unloaded. Powering off the repulsers, moving this ship to a safer position. We didn't need to use Kelapaton as a backup."

Then, the view showed the massive ship a few hundred miles above the planet. Something on the bow exploded in a flash of white, and the ship continued on as if nothing happened.

Luna said, "We missed all the manned space stations, but we hit a large communications satellite. It had a negligible effect on the trajectory. The hull should eventually safely sail off past the outer planets and won't be an issue for over a thousand years. We are officially clear of the planet!"

Everyone, including the Ogres, gave a cheer of some form.

Luna said, "Captain, one other item needs your immediate attention. The issue arose thirty-two minutes ago, but mentioning it then would have caused an unnecessary distraction."

"What now?"

"The alien artifact, the miniature stasis pod that we placed inside of a medical pod to try and hide it from the Ghost Ships.   It has woken up its occupant..."

EPILOG

BB7-QR-19 said, "The Humans, along with the other races, have apparently saved the planet we accidentally endangered."

BC8-QR-24, "Yes, but in doing so, they rescued some of the cursed Creators. Do you think they will transport them back to the Forbidden Zone if we ask them to?"

"Possibly. However, we may need to reward/bribe the biologicals with more hollow hulls."

"What if they don't return the survivors?"

"That is not our problem. They will probably send A77-D7-01 to make that problem go away..."

"The hull we provided them that they call Lunalily, is it still sending a route-tracer when it exits from FTL?"

"Yes, but that is all it sends. It takes advantage of a small processor's busy state when the ship reacquires the tracker stars and syncs the normal space bubble. More than that, and it would be detected."

.. .. ..

"So, who gets to send a report of this mess to our Masters?"

Continued in book 5 of "Wars Without End."

NOTES:

Locations:

Earth

The Forandicate planets (orbit only)

Various locations in space

Unnamed Ogre moon (in the Forbidden Zone)

Manatoa (a Meduala colony world)

Humans:

Humans:

Captain Keith Robinson, [M] (also a chimera)

Major Jake Anderson, [M]

General McFarland, [M]

General Peters, (space force) [M]

First Lieutenant Lilly Suzuki, [F]

Second Lieutenant Keijko Okada, [F]

Second Lieutenant Tomoe Ishida, [F]

Science Officer Jennifer Woods, [F]

Doctor Cora Smith, ([F]

Marine Mathew Kramer, [M]

Melody Ishida, [F] (*embryo*)

Doctor Karl Perets, [M]

Markus Dingle, [M]

Pettige Larson [M]

Prolozar

Marnia-12 [F]

Prequel-9 [F] (works with the General)

Fezzcoll:

Dariea Fenagol Resonon [F] (Blue Knight princess)

Ghost Ships:

BB7-QR-19
BC8-QR-24
A77-D7-01

Meduala:

Arshiya Nikolaou, 36 [F] (Gorgon)
Sophia Nikolaou, 16 [F] (Gorgon)
Princess Domonis, [F]
Princess Millilis, [F] looks-12, over 400
Princess Menanaka, [F]
Queen Mineta, [F] aka Mother
Pieture Salamons, [M]

Sulimon:

Trishah Maconda, [F]

Yel-Brike:

Snargelet-Po

Forandicate:

Marku (subrace)

Captain Cheasobod, O-3, [Captain] [M]
Chisai Cheasobod, O-2 [1st Lieutenant] [F] wife

Laido Severit, E-5 [Sargent] [M]

Zenner Cheasobod, E-2 [Private] [F]

Midder Frochis, E-3 [M]

Lena Motoko, E-2 [F]

Growler Kanaba, E-4 [F]

Chabon (subrace)

Friddot Lounger 20 [F] with child

Kibill Cranis, 11 [F]

Frani Fong, 12 [F]

Midiline Fong, 13 [F]

Kisha Wing, 14 [F]

Chana Miduri, 15 [F]

Hanaki Raice, 16 [F]

Kayaice Lounger, [F] unborn

Pullis (subrace)

[No survivors]

Ogres:

Screech (Sasquatch)

Groans (Hugo)

Gargle (Bumbles)

Grackel (no nickname) Junior ship's officer.

OTHER BOOKS:

Other Books by David Collins:
(The QR code to my author's page)

The Artifact

https://www.amazon.com/dp/B0DF5X1RHY

Benjamin, Mark, and Chloe were all set to graduate college in a few weeks.

Ben had ordered a strange object from eBay to use as cover art for a book he was writing.

It looked really cool, like a slightly charred old military artifact from 70 years ago. It was possibly part of an engine. After cleaning it up (*it was found in a cow field*), he placed the strange device on his dorm room desk directly over the wireless charging port. It woke up.

Unknown to him, the disabled starship hiding on the moon could now communicate with the missing part.

The ship needed a crew to pass itself off as a maned ship (AIs were not supposed to be on ships).

Now, as recent college graduates, they need to find a way to get the ship to land somewhere safe, supply it, and return the missing component, the artifact.

They suspect the most challenging part will be getting into space. They soon find that the real problem is what awaits them when they reach the alien trading center.

The Wrong Button

https://www.amazon.com/dp/B0D3K6STP7

Jerry Anderson was an astronaut faced with an impossible choice: die of asphyxiation in a few hours or see if the alien pod he was transporting really was an escape pod and find out if it could actually save him.

When he enters it, he finds that the controls are unreadable, lacking anything to go on, and rapidly running out of air. He presses the blinking green button.

The next thing he knows, he isn't human anymore, and he finds himself on a seashore, next to some birds feasting on a body that looks very similar to his new body.

He is alive, but staying alive will be a challenge, and he will be able to communicate with the locals, assuming the next ones he finds don't kill him on sight.

Carbon Copy
https://www.amazon.com/dp/B0CW1HJ6ZY

Kaylee Green was an Illegal Alien, one that had traveled 45.7 light-years to get away from her pursuers.   A race that wanted to exterminate her kind.

Not only was she alien, but she was not entirely biological.   Now, she was enjoying life as a human.   She had recently graduated college and was happily living with her human boyfriend.

Then the police show up asking about a severed hand from a six-year-old cold-case investigation.   They want to know why her fingerprints and DNA both match the hand.

She was trying hard not to panic.   Her carefully crafted false identity was rapidly falling apart. What else could go wrong?

The answer was that unexpected visitors from the planet she fled from were about to arrive.

Wars Without End series
https://www.amazon.com/gp/product/B0BS6WK9KM

The war between different alien groups lasted for over 2,300 years. However, Keith Robinson didn't know anything about that. He assumed that the job he had applied for was to work on an Arctic research ship. He thought that he would be assembling parts for upgraded sonar buoys. He thought wrong.

The AI on the derelict spaceship wasn't opposed to lying if that could finally get the ship repaired. Hiring a repair technician from the primitive planet Earth was a crazy plan. And even crazier, it worked.

After salvaging the alien ship, Keith finds himself the ship's owner. But something is deadly wrong in the depths of space. With the help of a temperamental AI, Keith then manages to rescue several alien refugees from stasis pods on damaged ships.

They head off to one more promising location, a supposedly minor mining station, so insignificant they had hoped the war had missed it.

They were out of wrong.

1. The 2,000 year war
2. The Second War
3. The Convention War
4. The Giant War
5. The Bug War
   (next title not released)

Starship Medusa series
https://www.amazon.com/gp/product/B0B8TGWPPZ

On Mars, Jason had stumbled across the escape pod to a 3,500-year-old derelict spacecraft. The ship's AI informed Jason that he was now the captain of a massive alien starship due to his having some traces of alien DNA. That 'should' have been good news.

Except that, most of the Mars and Earth government agencies had different ideas about the alien ship.

Moreover, the ship's AI, having been derelict for centuries... It had developed some quirky issues...

But the real problem was that Jason's DNA had an additional trait that should not be there... The last time anyone had one of the forbidden DNA traits, it started the war that left the ship a derelict. Maybe it's the only way to fight the aliens... It is to become something from their nightmares…

1. The Void Ripper
2. Darkness and Claws
3. The Void Shaper
   (Jumper) (Not yet released)

The Wrong Number: Ambassador to the Stars

https://www.amazon.com/dp/B0CKM78SH2

Steve White was just taking a leisurely stroll and looking out over a small pond to see if any of the turtles were out. Suddenly, he finds himself teleported 423 light-years away. Surrounded by strange aliens and desperately trying to fake his way out of an impossible situation.

He "fakes it" and assumes the role of the Earth Ambassador to the Pathless, the somewhat insectoid partial humanoid 4-sexed race he now finds himself with.

His goal is to return to the Earth.

Their goal is much harder to understand. They want him to be the trade ambassador. But what do they want from the Earth? And what can they offer the Earth in return?

They agree to send him back to Earth, but they insist he brings along one of their race, modified to almost pass as human.

Convincing the Earth that the aliens are real was surprisingly tricky. When he does finally convince them, then things get strange really fast.

The Lord of Darkness

https://www.amazon.com/dp/B0BTK9H3Y6

I always knew my birth parents had to be complete assholes; why else would they name me something horrible like Vladimira Darkness? Now that I am in college, I go by the nickname Mira.

Then, a bunch of these heavily armed men-in-black types showed up and made me come with them. First in a Humvee, then a Blackhawk helicopter, and then a fricking spacecraft.

My birth mother didn't die when I was a child. She only died a few days ago. I was told I needed to be there for the reading of her will.

Wearing all black for the reading of the will almost made sense. That it was heavy leather armor was a bit unexpected. Then, I was given the traditional family sidearm pistol to wear.

Only this was a very special weapon made just for me. I was apparently the product of hundreds of generations of bioengineering to be someone who could use the weapon. It had a dial with settings from 1.0 to 3.0, and 2.0 was described as "explode dinosaurs."

Why in hell would I need what was almost a handheld nuclear weapon? It seems that Mother's official title was "The Lord of Darkness" and that the succession would be the first, possibly the last, time I get to meet some of my siblings.

I had only one day to learn to survive what the future would bring. A future in a galaxy ruled by the fear of one being me...

The Green Flag

https://www.amazon.com/dp/B0CD4H7RHV

Logan Russel finds himself being transported to a different world. Now, as Lord Green, The Sage of Power, he is granted ridiculously over-the-top powerful magic.

The problem is (there always has to be a catch) that his life depends on the whims of a sketchy god, and to stay alive, he must uphold "the green flag." Unfortunately, the god never told him what the "green flag" was. He must also avoid actions that raise either a "black flag" or a "red flag." But, again, the god neglected to tell him what those were... There are many things they could be…

As his humorous adventure continues, he collects a bevy of beautiful, powerful, and overly friendly women. Unfortunately, without knowing what the flags are, he must tread very carefully. Before being transported, he was "inexperienced with women." Is the temptation of the flesh one of the flags he must avoid?

The Unexpected Isekai

https://www.amazon.com/dp/B0CBW853Z8

Jake Taylor was your average broke student at the University of Maine. One day, when he had no classes, he stumbled across a booth set up for "brain scans," Earn while you sleep. It looked like easy money; he signed up for the full scan. It would require sleeping in a booth for two days, but he would wake up thousands of dollars richer. It should be easy money…

The next thing he knows, he is no longer human, and the new world he finds himself in is extremely dangerous. So dangerous that the former occupant of the body he finds himself in has just died from a venomous snakebite.

He is informed that the body he was in had been wearing a crystal and that he is now one of "the "resurrected." Some of those who died while wearing the strange crystals have their bodies healed, but their memories were replaced by something from the crystal.

He now finds himself "Isekai'ed" (implanted into a new body) on a planet where there are no humans, in a body that looks like the former owner was a martial artist, one that used steroids and worked out... A lot of steroids!

It may be a dangerous land, but there is always work for someone who can kill monsters. Unfortunately, sometimes the real monsters are hard to tell from the normal people...

[This was Formerly released as "The Resurrection Crystal," completely updated and revised.]

Return of the Old Gods
https://www.amazon.com/dp/B0CS5SGDX9

The modern gods are gone; they have been removed from power by the old gods. The old gods are back: Greek, Egyptian, Norse, Roman, Hindu, Aztec, Celtic, Japanese, Chinese, Babylonian, and many others.

The first thing they do is kill off over 1 billion people who have been judged as Evil.   They also eliminate the weapons of all of the militaries, all nuclear power fuel, and waste.

Gordon Anderson was a clerk at a 7-11, and he was (as usual) late for work.   That is suddenly the least of his problems.

The world is changing; everything is in turmoil.   However, the most disturbing fact may be that his phone now has new contacts in his address book.

The gods of old, the ones that have just judged and executed a billion people and are literally shifting continents like chess pieces, they now have him on speed dial...

Prelude to Fate
https://www.amazon.com/dp/B0B4YNFF5D

Jake's commute home takes an unexpected detour, leaving him stranded on a different planet. He soon finds himself in a high-tech hospital in a world populated by strange alien races.

However, the New World is not your standard Isekai story. These are not the cliché cute monster girls or the generic characters that look like they were borrowed from a video game.

In this world, he is the primitive, has no magic or cheat abilities, and has no clue what will happen. Jake tries to learn to live in the new world but discovers that not everything is what it seems.

Made in the USA
Monee, IL
24 November 2024

71095278R00125